five GOLD rings

MO FANNING

Spring Street Books

First published by Spring Street Books Ltd 2020

Copyright © 2025 by Mo Fanning

ISBN: 978 099 3557 187

Book Cover by ABC

mofanning.co.uk | springstreetbooks.co.uk

For little children everywhere - no matter how old and cynical they've become

Dear reader

I always thought one day I'd feel inclined to bring together a handful of short stories written over the Christmas break. A time when I tend to be between writing one book and editing or publicising another.

And yes, I probably do sound like I'm terribly important using words like that, but it's really just a natural break in the year. I eat too much, used to drink too much (before I discovered I'm an alcoholic - who knew?) and watched too much rubbish telly. I often wrote a short story just to keep my hand in.

While procrastinating when I should have been writing my next book, I found a whole bunch of seasonal short stories, and decided to polish them up and bring you a different kind of Christmas anthology.

That Christmas Feeling

Josie reaches for Bertie's lead. Just like she has done every day around this time. For as long as she remembers. The tree is up, and the cupboards groan with food, but Josie can't bring herself to feel the Christmas season. Last night, she sat through a recording of carols, unmoved. The thought of the next two weeks fills her with dread.

Everyone at work brimmed with cheer. She joined in, donning a reindeer jumper and helping at the bake sale. She even stood on a chair to put up tinsel. Behind the fixed smile, there was sadness.

It's three weeks to the day she took her best friend for his final walk. Tomorrow will be the first Christmas in sixteen otherwise unremarkable years without Bertie.

Josie has done all she can to induce some seasonal spirit. She's downloaded *It's a Wonderful Life*. It always makes her cry. She'll watch it with the lights off and a box of fancy mince pies. If she keeps the room dark, Bertie might still be there, asleep in his basket—the one she hasn't yet moved from its rightful place in front of the gas fire.

The weather has been typically Christmas: rainy and dull. The sun broke through as the afternoon wore on, bathing the garden in golden light. Josie glanced at Bertie's lead, still hanging on the back of the kitchen door. At this time, she'd rattle her keys, and he'd leap from his basket to dance a jig at her feet.

She misses the walks, almost as much as she misses Bertie. Even though Josie lives alone, and doesn't hang out with people from work. The phone had rung twice during the week. Probably Carol from accounts, trying again to include her in Friday drinks.

Josie couldn't bring herself to answer.

She has dog-walking friends, and they'll have noticed her absence.

They'll have guessed Bertie is gone?

Unable to bear the silence any longer, she pulls on her coat.

Josie heads through the woods and smiles as she remembers how Bertie snuffled his way along the muddy path. She nods hello to Schnauzer Elaine and Labrador Bill. She can't bring herself to stop and chat because they'll ask about her best friend. Up ahead, someone sits on a bench. No dog at their side, and as she gets closer, she realises it's Poodle Pete.

'Hello, lovely lady,' he says, shuffling over for her to sit.

Josie hesitates.

Any minute now, Stinker will surely rush through the bushes, haa-haa-ing his way to chase a squirrel. She's uncertain she can cope with pretending there's nothing wrong.

'Are you all sorted for Christmas Day?' she asks.

'My Maureen has bankrupted us, and for what? It's only a big dinner.'

They sit in silence for a while, and when there's no sign of Stinker, she's forced to ask.

'Are you alone?'

He nods, and Josie's heart breaks. How could two of the loveliest boys leave this terrible world at the same time?

'I'm sorry,' she says and, overwhelmed by mute sadness, gets to her feet. 'I'd best head home. It'll be dark soon.'

'Three girls and a boy,' Pete says. 'I don't suppose you fancy seeing them?'

The walk to Pete's cottage takes only minutes, but already Josie feels lighter.

Stinker is the most attentive father. He fusses around Molly like he knows she's unsure where the four hungry balls of fluff came from.

'They're beautiful,' Josie says.

'That little black one,' Pete says. 'I bet he reminds you of someone.'

He does, and Josie has been doing her best not to notice. She's only got one picture of Bertie as a pup. He grew up so fast after leaving the rescue centre.

'We can't keep them,' Pete says. 'Come the new year, it's adoption time.'

All at once, Josie feels like Christmas—that warm and special glow that people try to bottle. She looks around Pete's front room and takes in the tree, the twinkling lights, the crackling logs on an open fire, and the smell of something lovely wafting from the kitchen.

'I could take him,' she says, quickly adding, 'that's if you don't mind. Obviously, I'll pay. Unless someone else has already got their name down...'

Later, Josie sits at home and smiles, sipping her sherry in the flickering light of the television screen. She dares herself to look over at Bertie's empty basket.

'You don't mind, lad?' she says.

And somewhere far away, she hears a grunty snuffle.
Like when she used to scratch his ears.
Or maybe it was the wind.
She can't be sure.
'Merry Christmas, old boy.'

Christmas 2.0

They call me 47B-stroke-9, which sounds like either a medical emergency or a particularly tedious tax form. I prefer my old name — Marcus — but that was before the Great Simplification of 2031, when the algorithm decided names were inefficient emotional baggage. The same algorithm, incidentally, that now runs our government and has inexplicably scheduled Christmas for the third Tuesday of every month.

'Festive productivity must be optimised,' it explains through the wall speakers as I queue for my regulation turkey-flavoured protein cube. The woman ahead of me — 33F-stroke-2, lovely cheekbones, terrible at small talk — argues with the dispensing unit about her lactose intolerance. The machine is having none of it.

'Dietary preferences are legacy code,' it informs her cheerfully, in that particularly grating synthetic voice that manages to sound both condescending and perpetually delighted. 'Please consume your allocated nutrition or face mandatory re-education.'

I've been through re-education twice. Once for suggesting that perhaps having Christmas twelve times a year somewhat dilutes its special quality, and once for what they called 'non-reproductive romantic preferences'. Being gay is acceptable only if you agree to monthly donations to the National Genetic Diversity Bank. I drew the line at displaying the accompanying promotional calendar. They can kink-shame as many test tubes as they like. I'm not giving it wall space.

The re-education centre, for those fortunate enough to have avoided it, is a beige building full of even beiger people showing PowerPoint presentations about 'optimal social harmony'. The chairs were designed by someone who clearly despised the human spine, and the tea is always just the wrong sort of lukewarm. Not cold, not hot — the temperature of surrender.

'Your deviation from standard behavioural patterns has been noted,' my re-education officer said, a man so bland I couldn't remember his face while looking directly at it. 'But the algorithm is merciful. The algorithm provides paths to redemption.'

'The algorithm can kiss my non-compliant arse,' I thought, but I decided to hold my tongue. Rumours were circulating about upgrades to the thought-crime sensors, and I wasn't entirely sure they couldn't pick up vehement internal monologues.

The decorations go up at precisely 6am every third Tuesday. Not gradually, with that delicious anticipation of old, but instantaneously via drone deployment. One moment you're looking at regulation grey walls, the next — boom — a red, green and silver explosion. It's like living inside a neglected branch of Lidl with a notably low-grade middle aisle.

The drones are ruthlessly efficient. I once witnessed one decorating a sleeping man on a park bench, and he woke having assumed the role of festive scarecrow. He tried to run, but the drones laced his legs together with tinsel. At the inevitable public inquiry, the Health and Safety Algorithm remained unamused.

'Happy Designated Celebration Period, 47B-stroke-9,' chirped my assigned Social Harmony Partner, 19C-stroke-6. Derek, he used to be called, back when we were allowed to fall in love rather than being matched by compatibility percentages. We scored 73%, which the algorithm assured us was satisfactory for long-term cohabitation with minimal conflict probability.

What the algorithm failed to account for was Derek's — sorry, 19C-stroke-6's — obsession with collecting vintage bathroom tiles and his belief that musicals are 'an authentic expression of the human condition'. Still, he's maintained his abs through three decades of regulation protein cubes, and has an arse like Michelangelo's David, and that counts for something. Rather a lot, if I'm being honest.

We met before the Simplification, in what used to be called a gay bar but is now designated as Social Interaction Venue 7-Lambda. Back then, it had disco balls and overpriced cocktails with suggestive names. Now it has efficiency-optimised lighting and serves something called Ethanol Solution Plus in regulation beakers. The music is composed by bots, trained on Hazell Dean and Steps. But lacking the fun of either.

Derek wore a shirt that said 'I'm not gay but my

boyfriend is,' which the algorithm now classifies as logically inconsistent humour, subcategory: deprecated. I bought him a drink — actual gin and tonic with real gin and over-priced organic tonic — and he laughed at my joke about the bartender's man bun looking like a hostage situation for his forehead.

'Remember when we could just meet someone and decide we liked them?' Derek said last week, during Designated Intimacy Hour.

'Careful,' I warned, glancing at the surveillance node in the corner that looked like a Christmas ornament but was actually recording everything for our monthly Relationship Efficiency Review.

'The tree's arrived,' he announces now, gesturing to the regulation 1.8-metre polyethylene spruce that materialised in our living cube via the mandatory goods chute. The same tree every month. We'd named it Sharon, though saying so out loud would trigger the Anthropomorphisation Sensors.

Sharon is a good tree, as regulation trees go. She's survived forty-three monthly Christmases, though she's starting to look a tad peaky. One branch has developed a permanent droop lending her a rakish, slightly intoxicated appearance. Derek insists this gives her character. The algorithm insists trees don't have anything that could be classed as character. We agree to disagree. Silently.

My work at the Bureau of Festive Compliance is exactly as soul-crushing as it sounds. My job involves reviewing citizens' mandatory Christmas cards for appropriate levels of cheer. Too much enthusiasm triggers the Emotional Excess protocols. Too little triggers the Insufficient Gratitude warnings. The sweet spot is a kind of tepid contentment, like finding a pound coin in an old coat pocket — pleasant... but not life-changing.

'This one's used an exclamation mark,' said my cubemate, 71D-stroke-3, whose previous name was either Jennifer or Jessica. I could never remember which, and she's been through re-education so many times she probably can't either.

'Flag it for review,' I say, not looking up from my own stack. Someone has drawn a Christmas tree that looks suspiciously penis-shaped. Creative subversion or genuine artistic incompetence? These are the decisions that haunt my regulation eight-hour work periods.

Our supervisor, 12A-stroke-1, walks past, his footsteps precisely metered to achieve optimal efficiency. He was Gerald once, I think, or possibly Gerard. He mutters, so I'm never sure. 12A-stroke-1 chose to embrace the Simplification with an enthusiasm that suggests either true belief or a nervous breakdown so complete it's come full circle to functionality.

And we all know how that goes, right?

'Productivity metrics are down 0.3% in this sector,' he announces to no one in particular. 'The algorithm is disappointed.'

'The algorithm can feel disappointment?' Jennifer-or-Jessica asks — which is brave of her.

'The algorithm feels everything and nothing,' 12A-stroke-1 replies, which would be deeply philosophical if it weren't delivered in the tone of someone reading a list of session musicians from a museum-piece Kate Bush album. 'It experiences optimal emotional equilibrium at all times.'

I wonder, not for the first time, if the algorithm is just a bunch of middle managers in a room somewhere, making increasingly absurd decisions to see how far they can push things before someone notices. Just how much piss can they actually take? The monthly Christmas thing certainly suggests a sick mind.

The Great Simplification didn't happen overnight. It crept in like damp in a basement flat — slowly, then all at once. First, it was just efficiency recommendations. 'Why have different wrapping paper designs when one will do?' Then came standardising celebration dates. 'Think of the supply chain optimisation!' Before we knew it, we were living in a world where spontaneity became an actual crime and joy was something scheduled for the third Tuesday of every month.

I remember the last real Christmas — December 2030. Derek and I spent it at his mother's cottage in the Cotswolds — back when the Cotswolds was more than Grid Reference 7-Alpha-9. She made actual roast turkey, the kind that came from a bird rather than a protein synthesis unit. We pulled crackers that contained terrible jokes we were allowed to groan at, wore paper crowns without Royalty Headgear permits, and got exactly as drunk as we wanted to be.

And that meant very drunk indeed. How else were we supposed to survive yet another *Mrs Brown's Boys* Christmas special?

'This is nice,' Derek's mother had said, looking at us over her third glass of actual wine. 'You two make sense together.'

The algorithm disagreed, initially. We only scored 68% on our first compatibility assessment. But there was still an appeals process back then, back when human opinion carried some weight. We argued that the algorithm hadn't factored in Derek's ability to make me laugh even during tax returns, or the way I apparently made his mother's infamous Christmas pudding 'almost edible' through creative use of brandy butter. And the fact I'm a size queen and Derek was blessed with an enormous penis.

Our appeal succeeded. We were granted *Cohabitation Permit 7-Gamma* with a probationary period of six months.

It was romance, algorithm-style.

This month's mandatory Secret Santa pairs me with 82A-stroke-5 from Productivity Sector 7. The gift options are: a grey scarf, a grey hat, or a grey mug with 'OPTIMAL CHEER' printed in slightly darker grey. I go with the mug.

Rebellion in the age of algorithms means choosing the least practical option.

82A-stroke-5 is ancient — possibly pre-Simplification ancient. She has the kind of face that suggests she's seen everything and found most of it wanting. During lunch breaks, she sits alone and knits — actual knitting with actual needles, which is technically illegal under the *Potential Weapons Act of 2032*, but no one is brave enough to tell her to stop.

'You know what I miss?' she said once, entirely unprompted, during a particularly grim February Christmas. 'Disappointing presents. Opening something and having to pretend you liked it. Your aunt's terrible perfume that smelled like a flower shop had been in a fight with a pharmacy. Those were the days.'

'You're not supposed to miss things,' I reminded her. 'Nostalgia is—'

'A form of temporal inefficiency, yes, I know.' She continued knitting what appeared to be either a scarf or a noose. With her, it was hard to tell. 'But the algorithm can't stop me remembering, can it? Not yet, anyway.'

She was right. The memory modification programmes are still in beta. Early trials result in people forgetting their own numbers, which causes all sorts of administrative headaches. One poor soul forgot the concept of Thursday entirely and had to spend a week living perpetually in Wednesday — which is almost poetic if you don't think too hard about it.

There are rumours of an underground resistance called the *December 25th Society*. They supposedly meet in secret to celebrate Christmas on its original date, with unauthorised decorations and non-regulation presents. Derek claims he's heard they even have actual mulled wine, though I suspect that's wishful thinking.

Derek is still fond of a tipple. As am I.

'My hairdresser's cousin knows someone who went to one of their meetings,' Derek whispered during our last *Designated Intimacy Hour*. The surveillance node was undergoing maintenance — a rare window of privacy.

'Your hairdresser has a cousin?' I asked.

Family relationships beyond immediate pairings have been discouraged since 2033.

'Had,' Derek corrected. 'Past tense. The cousin tried to organise a New Year's Eve party. On actual New Year's Eve.'

We both shuddered.

The last person to publicly celebrate New Year's Eve was made an example of. They were forced to watch a 72-hour PowerPoint presentation on 'The Arbitrary Nature of Calendar Systems' while sober.

The soberness was the cruel part.

I'm tempted to find this December 25th Society, but the risk is enormous. The algorithm has eyes everywhere — literally, in some cases. The new surveillance drones look like flying eyeballs, which someone in design thought was 'whimsically dystopian' rather than 'nightmare fuel'.

Still, the thought persists. Real Christmas. Once a year. Messy and inefficient and glorious.

The Christmas dinner is, as always, at precisely 18:00. Attendance is monitored via the subcutaneous tracking chips we all received as 'festive bonuses' in 2031. The cranberry sauce is purple this month — some glitch in the food synthesis programme that nobody could be bothered to fix. Or perhaps someone in Food Services is having their own quiet rebellion. Purple cranberry sauce is about as anarchistic as condiments could get.

Though I did once hear talk of green mayonnaise in what used to be known as Scotland. In a little town just outside Grid Reference 18-Omega-4.

The dining hall is a monument to regulation cheer. Identical tables with identical settings, each place marked with a number rather than a name. The crackers are pre-pulled to avoid the inefficiency of actual pulling, their contents (one grey paper crown, one approved joke, one plastic widget of no discernible purpose) laid out beside each plate.

'Remember,' the wall speakers remind us as we take our assigned seats, 'gratitude is mandatory, but excessive emotional display remains discouraged.'

I look around the regulation dining hall at hundreds of numbered humans wearing identical festive jumpers (this month's design: a minimalist reindeer that looks more like a malfunctioning coat hanger), mechanically pulling pre-pulled crackers and reading jokes approved by the *Humour Assessment Board*:

> *'Why did the chicken cross the road?*
> *To achieve its designated transportation*
> *objectives.'*

> *'What do you call Santa's helpers?*
> *Subordinate clauses.'*

That second one is actually almost funny, which means someone in the Humour Assessment Board is either slipping or subversive.

19C-stroke-6 reaches under the table and squeezes my hand — a tiny act of unsanctioned intimacy that could cost us both a week's protein cube ration if the sensors notice. They usually don't. Even algorithms, it seems, find enforced Christmas dinner remarkably boring.

To my left sits 94B-stroke-7, who was once a philosophy professor before the Simplification. He now works in Optimal Thinking Services, which is exactly as Orwellian as it sounds. He has the hollow-eyed look of someone who's thought too much about thinking and reached some terrible conclusions.

His name was Duncan. And we hooked up once or twice back when there was such a thing as a hook-up app.

He had a thing for golden showers, and I figured why not. It took a fortnight and six bottles of Zoflora to get the smell out of my bedroom rug.

'You know,' 94B-stroke-7 says quietly, moving regulation Brussels sprouts around his plate in a pattern that might be random or might be spelling out 'HELP' in Morse code, 'Sartre would have loved this.'

'How so?' I ask, genuinely curious. Philosophical discussions are discouraged but not explicitly banned, existing in that grey area the algorithm hasn't quite figured out how to police.

'Hell is other people,' he quotes. 'But he never imagined hell would have a spreadsheet and monthly performance reviews.'

Across from us, 33F-stroke-2 — the woman with the lactose intolerance — is staring at her regulation cheese substitute with the kind of intensity usually reserved for defusing bombs or understanding cryptocurrency.

'It's not even trying to be cheese,' she mutters. 'It's given up. It's the physical manifestation of surrender.'

'Citizen 33F-stroke-2,' the nearest speaker crackles, 'your food commentary has been noted. Please consume your allocated nutrition with appropriate gratitude.'

She picks up the cheese substitute, holds it to the light like a scientist examining a particularly disappointing specimen, and then, in a move that will later be called the *Dairy Defiance*, stood up.

'Merry Christmas,' Derek whispers, using my old name for the first time in years. 'Marcus.'

The wall speakers waste no time: 'Citizen 19C-stroke-6, you have committed a nomenclature violation. Please report for—'

But then, something extraordinary happens.

The lights flicker. The speakers cut out mid-sentence.

And somewhere in the distance, I swear I hear the sound of genuine, unsynthesised bells.

The woman with the lactose intolerance — 33F-stroke-2 — stands up and announces loudly: 'Sod this. My name is Patricia, and I want real bloody cheese.'

The silence that follows is the kind usually reserved for nuclear accidents or a *Royal-Significant* dying. Everyone stares at Patricia, waiting for the inevitable response from the algorithm. The enforcement drones should have been descending. The re-education alerts should have been screaming.

Nothing happens.

'The system's down,' someone whispers from the back of the hall. 'The whole network's crashed.'

82A-stroke-5, the ancient knitter, begins to laugh. Not the approved chuckle we're permitted during designated humour periods, but a proper, throaty guffaw that sounds like revolution.

'It was the purple cranberry sauce,' she wheezes between laughs. 'Someone in Food Services added a randomisation protocol to make it interesting. The algorithm can't process actual randomness. It's having the digital equivalent of a nervous breakdown.'

All around the hall, people get to their feet. Not in unison, not in any organised way, but in the beautiful, chaotic manner of humans remembering they were human.

'My name's Jennifer,' says my cube-mate.

'Gerald,' says our supervisor, looking slightly stunned. 'I was Gerald. I liked Gerard better, but my mother insisted on Gerald.'

Dodgy sex games Duncan stands on his chair, which

would have earned him a week's solitary productivity enhancement on any other day.

'If anyone's interested,' he shouts, 'I know where they keep the real alcohol.'

Derek grabs my hand, properly this time, not caring who sees.

'Marcus,' he says again, like he's tasting the word. 'God, I've missed saying that.'

'How long do we have?' I ask 82A-stroke-5, who seems to know more than she should about everything.

'The backup systems will kick in within an hour,' she says, already gathering her knitting. 'But an hour's enough to start something. The December 25th Society has been waiting for this. We've got safe houses, supplies, and seventeen years' worth of suppressed Christmas spirit ready to deploy.'

'You're part of the resistance?' Derek says.

'I founded it, dear.' She pulls what is definitely a noose from her knitting bag. 'Though this is for the algorithm's mainframe cables, not what you were thinking. Probably.'

What follows is the most gloriously inefficient hour in recent history.

Duncan does indeed know where the real alcohol is kept. It turns out the high-level administrators have been hoarding it for 'essential morale purposes'. We liberate several bottles of wine that have actual grapes in their ancestry, and someone finds a crate of beer that proclaims itself to be 'craft', though no one is entirely sure what that means anymore.

Patricia, the lactose revolutionary, leads a raid on the

kitchen stores. She finds a wheel of what might be actual cheddar. She eats it with the determination of someone making a political statement through dairy consumption.

'Form a queue!' someone shouts as we ransack the supplies, and then, 'Actually, don't! Don't form a queue! Mill about inefficiently!'

And we do. We mill. We meander. We move in patterns that would have given the algorithm a digital aneurysm. It is beautiful.

Derek finds a guitar somewhere — God knows where, musical instruments were relegated to *Historical Archive Centres* in 2034. He plays Christmas songs, the old ones, the ones that made no sense about figgy pudding and good kings looking out. And how *all he wants for Christmas is you*. By which, I assume he means me.

Half of us have forgotten the words, but we sing anyway, making up lyrics that are absolutely not approved by any board or committee.

'Jingle bells, algorithm smells, surveillance flew away,' sings Jennifer, already three glasses into the leadership wine and swaying like one of those inflatable tube men you used to see on American telly shows. Back when there was telly. And America.

Someone starts a conga line. The last person to attempt synchronised non-productive movement was sent to *Kinetic Efficiency Training* for a month. But here we are, a human chain of beautiful inefficiency, snaking through the dining hall while Duncan quotes Nietzsche at the top of his voice.

'Forty minutes,' 82A-stroke-5 announces. She produces a pocket watch from somewhere, an analogue one that the algorithm can't track. 'We need to start moving people to safe houses.'

'Where?' I say.

'The old Tesco on Richmond Road. We've been converting the basement into a Christmas bunker. We've got decorations from the 2020s, actual mince pies — though they're well past their sell-by date — and a DVD of *Die Hard*.'

'*Die Hard*?' Derek's eyes light up. 'The Christmas film?'

'The only Christmas film that matters,' she replies solemnly.

We split into groups. Patricia leads one faction to raid the maintenance supplies for anything that could be repurposed as decorations. Duncan takes another group to liberate more alcohol, because revolution without wine is just inefficient violence, and we've had enough efficiency for several lifetimes.

Derek and I are assigned to what 82A-stroke-5 called 'Operation Santa's Sack' — rescuing any personal items people hid that reminds them of the before times. It turns out everyone has something. Jennifer has a photo of her old cat, Mr Whiskers, hidden inside her regulation pillow. Gerald has a Pokémon card — Charizard, first edition — that he's kept sealed in plastic for twenty-three years.

'It's stupid,' he says, clutching it like a religious relic. 'But my son gave it to me. Before the Family Optimisation Protocol separated us.'

Nothing about it is stupid. In a world that tries to strip meaning from everything, the stupid things are the only things that matter.

'Thirty minutes,' 82A-stroke-5 calls. 'Time to go.'

But Patricia isn't done. She's found the decorations storage, where all the monthly Christmas supplies are kept. Thousands of identical trees, millions of regulation baubles, enough tinsel to wrap the world in not-quite-silver monotony.

'Burn it,' she says. 'Burn it all.'

'That seems a bit extreme,' Gerald ventures.

'You're right,' Patricia agrees. Then she grins, and it's the grin of someone who found their calling. 'Let's redecorate it all first, then burn it.'

We have twenty minutes left when we hear them coming. Not the algorithm — it's still having its digital crisis — but the manual override forces. The people who've drunk so deeply from the well of optimisation that they've forgotten they were ever once people at all.

'Citizens,' their leader calls through a megaphone that somehow manages to make his voice even more monotonous than usual, 'you are in violation of seventeen efficiency protocols and at least three happiness mandates. Return to your designated positions for processing.'

'Process this!' Patricia shouts, and throws a wheel of possibly-cheese at his head. It misses, but the thought is there.

We run. Not in an organised fashion, not in optimal evacuation patterns, but in the glorious chaos of humans who remember what it's like to be human. Derek grabs my hand and we sprint through corridors we've walked through at regulation pace for years, our footsteps echoing like drums, like music, like freedom.

82A-stroke-5 is surprisingly fast for someone of her vintage. She leads us through a service tunnel I didn't know existed, her knitting needles tucked behind her ears like deadly hair accessories.

'I mapped these tunnels in 2031,' she explains as we crawl through spaces definitely not designed for optimal human transit. 'The algorithm never bothered with them because they were inefficient. That's the thing about perfect systems — they can't imagine why anyone would choose the imperfect path.'

Behind us, the manual override forces try to follow, but have to keep stopping to file reports about the safety violations they're committing by entering non-standard passages. Bureaucracy, it turns out, can work both ways.

We emerge into the old Tesco car park, where dozens of others are already gathering. The December 25th Society has been busy. There are actual Christmas lights strung between the abandoned lamp posts, wonky and beautiful. Someone has built a snowman out of packing foam and given it a carrot nose. An actual carrot.

'Welcome,' says a man I recognise as 15C-stroke-3 from Waste Management, 'to the real Christmas.'

The basement of the old Tesco is like stepping into a time machine operated by someone with a serious tinsel addiction and questionable taste in Christmas jumpers. There are decorations from every era — 1970s aluminium trees, 1980s singing Santas, those projection lights from the 2010s that made your house look like it had festive chickenpox.

'We've been collecting for years,' 82A-stroke-5 explains, settling into an armchair that has seen better decades. 'Every time they destroyed something, we saved a piece. It's not pretty, but it's ours.'

Derek found the DVD player and set up *Die Hard* on a TV that required percussive maintenance to maintain colour.

'Look,' he says, 'Bruce Willis has a green tinge, but if you squint, it's festive.'

Patricia appoints herself chief of non-regulation food distribution. She'd found tins of things that didn't even exist anymore — Quality Street chocolates that are actually different from each other, cranberry sauce that's decidedly not purple, and something claiming to be 'Aunt Bessie's Yorkshire Puddings' that probably violates several current food-shape regulations.

'The algorithm will reboot eventually,' Gerald says, but he's wearing a paper crown at a jaunty angle that suggests he didn't much care.

'Let it,' Patricia replies through a mouthful of potentially illegal cheese. 'We've got three weeks until actual Christmas. December 25th. The real one.'

'What then?' I ask.

82A-stroke-5 smiles, and it's the smile of someone who's been planning this for a very long time.

'Then, my dear Marcus — yes, I know your real name, I've known all of you since before the numbers — then we remind everyone what it's like to celebrate something because we want to, not because we're told to.'

I'm writing this on actual paper, with an actual pen that Derek found in the museum of inefficient communication devices (formerly known as WH Smith or whatever they renamed it after that).

The algorithm rebooted, of course. It always does.

But something had changed.

The purple cranberry sauce incident, as history will probably remember it, exposed a fatal flaw in the system. Perfect efficiency couldn't account for human chaos. The algorithm could process our compliance, but it couldn't process our joy.

The December 25th Society went public. Well, as public as you can go when public assembly was still technically illegal. We celebrated Christmas — real Christmas — in the basement of that Tesco. There were seventy-three of us, each with our names, our actual names, written on badges made from cereal boxes.

The manual override forces found us, naturally. They stood at the entrance to our basement kingdom, looking at the chaos of mismatched decorations, the people singing off-key carols, Duncan the philosophy professor doing an interpretive dance to 'Good King Wenceslas' that would have made Nietzsche weep.

'This is inefficient,' their leader said, but his heart wasn't in it.

'Yes,' 82A-stroke-5 agreed. 'Gloriously, beautifully, perfectly inefficient. Would you like a mince pie? They're probably toxic by now, but that's rather the point.'

He took the mince pie.

That's how revolutions really work — not with grand gestures, but with small acts of defiance that taste of cinnamon and questionable preservatives.

The algorithm still runs things, officially. We still have our numbers, still have monthly Christmas imposed from above.

But there are cracks now — beautiful cracks where humanity seeps through.

The purple cranberry sauce appears more often.

The jokes in the crackers are actually funny.

Sometimes, just sometimes, someone uses a real name and the speakers pretend not to notice.

Derek and I are still together, still scoring our suboptimal 73% that somehow equals 100% in all the ways that matter. And his arse... it still causes marvel in me.

Patricia opened an illegal cheese shop in her living room. Gerald reunited with his son through an 'administrative error' that 82A-stroke-5 definitely had nothing to do with, honest.

And Duncan - well he's become very close to another gentleman. Clive. Who looks fabulous in yellow rubber.

And every December 25th, we gather. Not because we're told to, not because it's efficient, but because we choose to. We sing the old songs badly, exchange presents wrapped in newspaper, and watch *Die Hard* on that green-tinged TV.

The algorithm watches us, I'm sure. But perhaps, just perhaps, somewhere in its vast digital consciousness, it's learning something that can't be optimised or processed or made efficient: that the most perfect system is the one that admits its own imperfection.

Or maybe it's just biding its time until it can force us to celebrate Easter seventeen times a year.

With the algorithm, you never really know.

But for now, in this moment, my name is Marcus. His name is Derek. And tomorrow, whatever day it is, won't be Christmas unless we say it is.

The revolution isn't over. It's just begun. And it tastes like possibly-cheese and definitely rebellion.

Number 47B-stroke-9 is currently enjoying his thirty-seventh consecutive life sentence for 'aggravated nostalgia', 'distribution of non-regulation narratives', and 'possession of actual cheese with intent to distribute'. He remains optimistic about parole, though he's hidden this manuscript in a place the algorithm will never think to look — inside the technical manual for optimal happiness. No one ever reads that.

Confessional

Bev had been driving the emergency locksmith van for three years, but Christmas Eve was always the worst. Not because of the cold - though Manchester in December could freeze your eyeballs solid - but because of the stories. The maudlin, mawkish stories. Everyone locked out on Christmas Eve had a tale to tell, and they all wanted to share it with Bev while she worked.

'Right then,' she said, pulling up outside a terraced house in Chorlton where the front door mocked her from afar. 'Let's see what you've got in store for me.'

The woman stood waiting on the doorstep was about forty, wearing reindeer pyjamas and slippers shaped like Santa heads. The kind of person who thought herself quirky. If you ran into her at any sort of office Christmas party, she'd be the one pulling on your arm, insisting you should dance.

'Mrs Middleton?' Bev said, setting her tool bag down.

'Linda. And thanks for coming so fast. The turkey's in the oven and my mother-in-law is due in an hour.'

Bev nodded and set to work.

'I could kill him,' Linda muttered as she paced up and down trying to get warm. Bev had a spare coat in the van, she ought to offer to fetch it.

'Husband?' Bev asked. 'I bet he's at work, blissfully unaware.'

'Try passed out on the bloody sofa. Pissed as a fart.'

Bev heard this more often than you might think. She sized up the Yale lock. 'Shouldn't be much longer, Linda. You can sit in my van if you like.'

'The thing is,' Linda continued, because they always continued, 'I did it on purpose.'

Bev's drill paused. 'Come again?'

'I locked myself out on purpose. I was standing there in my kitchen, looking at that bloody great turkey. Cost forty-three quid. And I thought, "I can't do this anymore."' Linda's voice cracked. 'Twenty-three years of Christmas dinners. Twenty-three years of his mother telling me my roast potatoes are soggy and my gravy's too thin. Twenty-three years of him falling asleep in his chair while I clean up.'

The lock gave way with a satisfying click.

'So I came out here and let the door slam shut. Thought maybe if I couldn't get back in, Christmas would just... not happen.'

Bev began putting away her tools. 'But you called me.'

Linda wiped her nose with her sleeve. 'Yeah, well. The neighbours were staring.'

Bev stepped aside. 'You are alright, though Mrs Middleton?'

'I said to call me Linda and yeah. I suppose you have to be, don't you?'

When she paid, she insisted Linda take a tenner extra for her trouble. Money for a drink. Or whatever.

Her next call was to a flat above a chippy in Hulme. Young lad, maybe twenty-five, standing in his boxers and a Manchester City shirt despite the frost.

'Alright, love?' he called down from the third-floor window. 'I'm Kai. Bit of a situation up here.'

Bev climbed three flights of stairs that smelled of stale fat and winter rot. Kai's door was solid wood, double-locked.

'Emergency locksmith,' she announced.

'I know, I called you. It's just... well, it's a bit embarrassing.'

'I've seen it all, love.'

'I locked myself out running away from my girlfriend.'

'Right.'

'Ex-girlfriend now, I suppose. She was wrapping presents on the bed. Christmas presents for her kids from her previous relationship. And she asked if I wanted to help. Kids I've never met, right? And I just... panicked. Grabbed my keys and ran for it. But the door slams shut, doesn't it, and now all my stuff's in there with her.'

Bev stared at Kai. 'You didn't think of knocking?'

His face turned a delicious shade of red. 'She told me to get stuffed.'

Bev knelt to find the right drill and set to work on the lock.

'What kind of presents?' she said, having never been one for empty air.

'What?'

'The kids. What was she wrapping for them?'

Kai shifted on his bare feet. 'Lego. One of them Star Wars sets. And some books. Harry Potter, I think.'

'How old are they?'

'Eight and eleven.'

'Boys or girls?'

'One of each. Listen, why does this matter?'

Bev got the first lock open, started on the second. 'Just wondering what kind of woman buys Star Wars Lego and Harry Potter books for Christmas.'

'A good one,' Kai said quietly.

'And you ran away because…?'

'Because I'm a dickhead who's terrified of being responsible for anyone else's happiness.'

The lock clicked open.

'There you go,' Bev said. 'Door's open. Your ex-girlfriend's probably still up there wrapping presents for kids who'll be over the moon Christmas morning because someone cares enough to get them exactly the right thing.'

Kai stared at the open door like it might bite him.

Bev wanted to give him a shove and tell him to stop acting the fool. That some people would be happy to have somebody—anybody, really. No matter if they were wrapping gifts for kids from their ex.

She held her tongue. She always did.

The final job of her shift was a nursing home in Withington. The night manager, a tired-looking woman in her fifties, met her at the front door.

'Thanks for coming out. It's our medicine cabinet. Lock's jammed, and we've got residents who need their evening medications.'

Bev followed her down corridors that smelled of disinfectant, past a lounge where a dozen elderly people sat watching *It's a Wonderful Life* with the sound turned up too loud.

'Busy night?' the manager asked as Bev examined the cabinet lock.

'Always is, Christmas Eve. People do daft things when they're emotional.'

'Tell me about it. We had three family rows just this afternoon. Grown children arguing over who's taking Mum home for Christmas dinner, meanwhile Mum just wants to stay here and watch telly in peace.'

The lock was more corroded than jammed. Bev worked carefully. Medicine cabinet locks needed to stay secure once she'd fixed them.

'That's the thing about Christmas,' the manager continued. 'Brings out the best and worst in people. The guilt, the expectations, the pressure to be happy.'

'You working tomorrow?'

'Course. Someone has to. Half the staff have families to get back to.' She paused. 'What about you?'

'Me?' Bev concentrated on the lock. 'Haven't got family.'

'Friends?'

'Not the Christmas dinner type.'

The mechanism clicked back into place, smooth as silk.

'Fixed,' she said, testing it a few times.

'Brilliant. Here, before you go—' The manager disappeared into an office and returned with a plate covered in foil. 'Leftover Christmas cake from our party earlier. Homemade.'

Bev was about to refuse, but something in the woman's expression stopped her. 'Ta very much.'

Walking back to her van, she heard singing from the lounge. The residents must have grown tired of angels getting their wings and found a carol service. Their voices were thin, but they knew every word.

Back home in her bedsit above the launderette, Bev made a cup of tea and unwrapped the Christmas cake. It was heavy with fruit and soaked in brandy, the kind that took weeks to make properly. She ate a slice, thinking about Linda in her reindeer pyjamas, standing outside her own front door trying to escape Christmas. About Kai in his boxers, too scared to love someone else's children. About the night manager, spending Christmas Day making sure other people's parents were looked after.

She thought about her van, filled with tools for getting people back into the places they'd locked themselves out of. Sometimes accidentally, sometimes on purpose.

Her phone buzzed. Text message.

Emergency call-out Stockport.

Family locked out, baby crying

Christmas presents in car.

Can you cover?

Bev looked at the Christmas cake, at her empty bedsit, at the rain starting to streak down her single window.

She texted back to take the job.

It was double time, after all—money to save for another rainy day.

Twenty minutes later she was driving through the dark streets of Manchester, Christmas lights blinking in windows, her van loaded with tools for fixing the small disasters people created when they were trying to love each other, or trying to avoid it, or sometimes just trying to survive another day.

Behind every locked door, someone was waiting to get back in. Or counting the hours until they could get out. Her radio crackled to life.

'Bev? Got another one for you if you're interested. Chorlton way.'

She recognised the address immediately.

'I'll take it,' she said, turning the van around.

When she pulled up outside Linda's house, she could see through the front window. The dining room table was set for four, candles lit, crackers laid out. And Linda sat on the doorstep again.Same reindeer pyjamas. This time the door stood open.

'Alright, love?' Bev called, winding down her window. 'Think our system might be buggered. They've sent me back here.'

Linda looked up and grinned. 'I'm just sitting here for a bit. Watching the world go by.'

'On Christmas Eve? In your pyjamas?'

'Why not? It's my house, isn't it?'

Bev parked up and got out. 'How'd dinner go then?'

'Mother-in-law loved the potatoes. Said they were the best she'd ever had.' Linda laughed. 'Husband woke up, helped with the washing up. Miracles do happen.'

'How come you're sitting out here in the cold?'

Linda was quiet for a moment. 'Just thinking about that locksmith who came earlier. Wondering what she was doing for Christmas.'

Bev felt something warm and unexpected settle in her chest.

'Fancy a cup of tea?' Linda asked. 'I've got Christmas cake.'

'I've already had some tonight.'

'Well then, you know what they say about buses.'

Bev looked at Linda sitting on her doorstep like she owned the world, at the warm light spilling from her house, at the street full of homes where people were having the same minor disasters and small triumphs that made up Christmas everywhere.

'Go on then,' she said, locking up the van. 'But I'm not staying long. People need their doors fixed.'

'Course not,' Linda said, standing up and brushing frost off her reindeer pyjamas. 'Just long enough for a proper cup of tea.'

They went inside together, leaving the front door wide open.

Sometimes the best way to be home is to know you could leave anytime you wanted.

But choose not to.

Evergreen Close

According to a report by the local council, Evergreen Close had maximised community inclusion through targeted regeneration and sustainability initiatives. An estate agent might have used different words while selling one of the three remaining units. Taylor and Sons' website described them as 'stunning four-bedroom detached properties on a prestigious new development on the outskirts of town'. They were built to an exceptional standard and exuded contemporary style and quality craftsmanship.

The Smiths and the Joneses lived next door to each other at numbers 16 and 18 Mulberry Close, in homes with spacious entrance halls, open-plan kitchen/diners, and four good-sized bedrooms. Both families cherished their ample parking and the ten-year NHBC warranty on their homes.

Mrs Smith always said good morning to Mrs Jones. Mr Smith nodded the occasional hello to Mr Jones. Their kids didn't mix. The Smiths sent their children to a private school, while the Joneses made do with the local school that had just become an academy.

They had moved into their homes at the end of summer, so neither family could have known how the other might deal with Christmas. Mrs Smith knew her husband had a competitive streak. Mrs Jones worried her husband didn't like to be beaten at anything.

It was always going to happen.

The Smiths set about upgrading their superb new-build home in an idyllic position on a quiet cul-de-sac within days of taking possession. They replaced the lawn with artificial grass and widened their drive to accommodate two towering SUVs and a high-end motorbike. The Joneses left everything much as they found it. Mr Jones cleaned windows for a living and drove a white van. Mr Smith called Mr and Mrs Jones unambitious. But still, they nodded hello when they passed, and life continued.

And then December dawned...

Mr Smith, who wore his arrogance like a too-tight festive jumper, came home one evening to find Mr Jones had garlanded his tatty little van with blinking lights and a red-nosed reindeer decal. And that wasn't all. The high-performance uPVC double-glazed windows — which allowed ample natural light into the living space — were peppered with neon snowflakes.

Over a Marks & Spencer Gastropub meal, Mr and Mrs Smith prepared their counterattack.

'A tree,' Mr Smith said. 'One that says we mean business.'

Mrs Smith speared a minted new potato. 'I'm not hoovering up needles.'

'Not a real one,' he said, in a voice that suggested his wife might be losing her marbles. 'I'll make some calls and find out who supplies our local shopping centre.'

And that was how it started. A few neon snowflakes, a reindeer red nose, and a tree.

By the middle of December, Evergreen Close—once quiet and unassuming—blinked and buzzed with a cacophony of festive lights and electronic melodies. The Smiths' front garden was a riot of colour, a blinding beacon of tasteless cheer, with inflatables jostling for space like rush-hour commuters. On the other side of an all-weather fence, the Joneses' display was an orchestra of similar excess, every twinkling light synchronised to the plunk-plonk-ping of 'Winter Wonderland'. LED snowmen stood like soldiers, and fairy lights became barbed wire between festive foes.

The air was thick with artificial pine and electronic cheer, a synthetic symphony that drowned out the natural peace of the season.

But neither family would admit this was any sort of competition. Draped in garish Christmas jumpers, Mr and Mrs Smith and Mr and Mrs Jones stood in their respective gardens, offering saccharine smiles and hollow compliments.

'Shame nobody else wants to put in any effort,' Mrs Smith said, nodding across the way to where Mrs Green's house still had the same manicured front lawn, the same pre-planted conifers, and the same beige show-home curtains as when she moved in. Mrs Green kept herself to herself. She drove a battered Fiat 500 and was almost always out somewhere.

And then the council announced a competition. For the best-decorated house. With the prize to be awarded on Christmas Eve.

Vans delivered boxes, bags, parcels, and items arriving on pallets daily. Mrs Jones saw Mrs Smith in Sainsbury's buying an inflatable Santa. She waited until the coast was clear and bought two.

Christmas Eve arrived. The Smiths unveiled a sleigh with real reindeer, while the Joneses countered with a live Nativity scene, complete with a donkey that began eating a nearby hedge.

The man from the council was due at 6 pm, so both families got into position. The nodding hello thing was long forgotten.

By 7:15, Mr Jones suggested it might be OK for Mrs Jones to nip inside and use the loo—but only if it was number twos, and only if she promised to be quick. They couldn't have the inspector arrive and find Mary missing from the scene. She was, he pointed out, central to the story.

By 8 o'clock, as stars twinkled in the night sky, an uncommon stillness descended upon the street. Mrs Smith glanced over at Mrs Jones and shrugged. She smiled back as if to say that maybe, just maybe, things had gone too far.

Across the road, Mrs Green climbed into her car. A tatty tinsel tree stood in her front window, and now, just as the prize announcement was about to happen, she was leaving.

Mr Smith turned a shade of red that rivalled the nose on Mr Jones's van.

'Hey,' he called out. 'You there. We're about to find out who won the prize.'

Mrs Green did her very best to smile.

'Does it matter?' She sounded weary.

'Of course it bloody well matters. This is important. We've spent an absolute fortune on making sure we win. This could put Evergreen Close on the map.'

Mr Jones came to join in. 'Where are you off to, anyway? It's Christmas bloody Eve. The shops are all shut.'

Mrs Green glanced at the glittering tableau. 'I'm afraid there's somewhere I need to be.'

'Can't it wait?' boomed Mr Smith. 'This is important. It could do wonders for property prices.'

She shook her head. 'It really can't wait.'

And Mrs Green got into her car and drove away. She didn't even beep her horn, wave, or wish either family good luck. Her brake lights blinked at the end of the close, and then she was gone.

'Snotty cow,' said Mrs Smith.

'Up herself mare,' agreed Mrs Jones.

The man from the council never came. And at 9:30, both families turned off the lights and headed back inside. Mr Smith poured himself a tot of fine whisky. Mr and Mrs Smith opened what should have been their celebratory champagne. It tasted sour.

Mrs Green didn't come home that night. Not that anyone noticed in the Smith and Jones homes. She didn't come home the next day. Nor the one after that. The lights in her house stayed dark. The tinsel tree looked lonely.

Angry phone calls to the Council Christmas Garden helpline went unanswered, so both the Smiths and the Joneses set to dismantling their displays.

On a gloomy, cold December morning, as Mr Smith gathered up a tangled mess of extension leads, he caught sight of Mr Jones bundling up neon reindeer. Their eyes met briefly before both looked away. He wanted to tell his neighbour he was sorry things got out of hand. But he couldn't. Not yet, anyway.

Mrs Smith sauntered across the road to check on Mrs

Green. Mrs Jones followed. They stood in silence for a moment, realising how caught up they had been in their petty competition.

'Her daughter was sick,' Mrs Jones said. 'I heard someone talking about how she was in hospital.'

Mrs Smith nodded. 'That explains it. Perhaps she's staying over. They let you do that in some hospitals. The Millscroft has superb guest accommodation. Have you ever been?'

Mrs Jones shook her head. Of course she hadn't been to the big private hospital on the edge of town. She wasn't made of bloody money.

Two days later, Evergreen Close finally learned what had happened to their neighbour. Police arrived bearing the tragic news—her car had been struck by a lorry on Christmas Eve.

Investigators determined the accident occurred when a giant inflatable Santa from an overzealous light display on Willow Lane had broken free and blown across the road, causing the lorry to swerve. She died instantly.

The Smiths and the Joneses stood in the street as the words sank in. Obscene holiday rivalry had led to an innocent woman losing her life.

The festive fever that once held Evergreen Close in its garish grip slowly dissipated as the bleak midwinter sun rose over the day after Christmas. A profound and resonant silence fell over the neighbourhood — a stark contrast to the cacophony of the previous weeks.

Standing amidst the remnants of their once extravagant display, the Smiths struggled to process the tragic news delivered by sombre-faced officers. Mrs Smith's fingers trembled as she removed a glittering ornament from the artificial tree, her eyes no longer gleaming with competitive fire.

Beside them, the Joneses appeared equally subdued, the echoes of their former rivalry now distant and petty. Mr Jones unplugged a string of lights, silencing the synthetic melodies and leaving room for a sorrowful reflection that hung in the air like their frosty breath.

The competitive zeal that had propelled them into an arms race of holiday spirit was replaced by a shared sense of guilt and an unspoken question had the pursuit of one-upmanship contributed to the accident? Had their desire to outdo each other blinded them to the real joys and meaning of the season? It could so easily have been one of their inflatable Santas.

In the days that followed, a transformation occurred on Evergreen Close. The decorations were put away—not with thoughts of what might happen next year, but with vows of remembrance and change. The once-bright gardens stood bare and reflective under the winter sky.

Once divided by petty one-upmanship, the Smiths and Joneses stood united in grief. They shared a bond of tragedy and a responsibility to do something better. Together, they agreed to forgo the grandeur of future Christmas competitions in honour of Mrs Green and instead focus on fostering a true sense of community.

Each December, on the anniversary of their quiet neighbour's untimely passing, Evergreen Close came alive with the glow of candles and the warmth of shared memories. There were no twinkling lights or festive inflatables. The residents gathered not to outshine each other but to share in the spirit of togetherness, reflecting on the year gone by and the preciousness of time.

And so, through a collective commitment to remember

and honour, the people who bought the stunning four-bedroom detached properties of Evergreen Close discovered that the brightest lights shone from a community united, not in rivalry, but in the heart of true holiday spirit.

And the council banned inflatables.

Fling Nothing Skywards, OK?

'I've gone six months without needing to socialise, Maureen. Why would Christmas change that?'

I'd asked a fair question, and my social worker pulled a face before writing something in her notes, clicking the top of a four-coloured biro and sitting back in what used to be Frank's armchair.

'In which case, we'll see each other again in the new year, Flo.'

At the front door, she couldn't decide how best to say goodbye.

'January 3rd,' she said, as she took off her mask and blew a kiss.

As she drove away, the horn beeped, but I'd already closed the front door.

In the kitchen, I switched on Radio 4.

The woman reading the news sounded northern. It's a thing with the BBC—regional voices. Yesterday, the weather presenter had such a strong Geordie accent that I struggled to understand the forecast. Today's headlines reported how our straw-headed scarecrow of a prime minister was going to fix things so Christmas need not be cancelled. In exchange, we were to get one extra lockdown month in January.

None of that bothered me.

Lockdown gave me the perfect excuse not to spend Christmas Day in Julia and Neil's overheated, dull home. No smiling through her too-dry turkey and undercooked sprouts. No dull-as-ditchwater game of Monopoly, and best of all, no grandchildren singing Christmas bloody carols.

I posted their presents. Five-pound notes pinned into cards.

I hoped they wouldn't get nicked.

It was on the news that the Post Office were having to fire kids for stealing letters. Because of the pandemic, everyone was sending money.

There was a knock, and I looked up from my crossword.

'Come in, Robert,' I said. 'Don't stand on ceremony.'

He was a pleasant lad. Mid-twenties, and he understood how to speak to the older generation. He treated me with respect. None of that speaking slowly or shouting as though I might be deaf or unable to work Netflix.

'How about a cup of tea, Flo?' he said, and before I could answer, he filled the kettle and reached down cups.

Bone china. A wedding present.

At the time, I'd lied to everyone about their gorgeous appearance. They're not. I hate yellow, but Frank's parents bought us a full dinner service: six plates, six side plates, six bowls, six cups, and six saucers. All in yellow.

I switched my attention back to solving two across. Fling nothing skywards, OK? Six letters.

'These are lovely,' Robert said. 'I love drinking from a proper cup.'

'You're welcome to have them.'

He looked at me like I'd said the strangest thing ever. He opened the fridge for milk.

'This smells a bit dodgy, Flo,' he said. 'You should get some more before the shops shut for Christmas.'

My name was Florence, and Flo sounded like an old lady's name. Except somehow, I didn't mind with Robert. He was a likeable lad. We met when he turned up at my door and asked if I needed any odd jobs doing. I laughed and said he looked a bit old for a Boy Scout, but yes, I had things to tackle around the house and garden. He charged me next to nothing to dig out a tree stump, prune my hedge, and fish a dead pigeon from the loft.

In any other story, Robert would be a 'bad seed', secretly robbing me blind.

You couldn't be more wrong.

'Will I stay on after I finish in the garden?' he always said, changing his voice each time he asked.

I'd ask if he wanted to stay, and he'd say yes.

Robert liked to smoke in bed. I considered it an unpleasant habit and tried to get him to stop, but I forgave him anyway.

'Cigarettes are bad for your health,' I often said.

'Live for the day,' he'd shoot back with a grin.

'I suppose you'll be with your family,' I said, and when he didn't answer right away, I knew my answer.

'If there was any other way...'

'Stop talking.' I held up my hands. 'You should be with little Emma.'

I shuffled down into the bed, pulling the duvet up around my face, and he snuck across the landing to use the loo.

Dry turkey, congealed gravy, something that might pass

for a potato, poor lighting, and liquid sprouts. One cracker. One mince pie.

'What am I supposed to do with this?' I said when the girl handed me the tray.

She smiled. 'Merry Christmas, Flo.'

I told her I was Jewish and slammed the door in her smug do-gooder face.

Robert phoned mid-morning, sounding like he was outside. I fancied a nice long chat, but he said he couldn't stay long. Julia was next, and she put me on speaker-phone so I could hear Aaron and Amber share the harmonies on 'Hark the Herald Angels Sing'.

Robert had taught me how to work the mute button, so I screamed, 'Get fucked,' and poured a second vodka.

They were very kind when they came. I wasn't sure how quickly they might respond what with it being Christmas Eve. And as I explained on the phone ... it wasn't as if they'd be able to do much. The girl sat with me and asked if I wanted to call anyone. Was there someone I could be with? I just shook my head and said I was fine on my own. I insisted she head off and help other people. People who hadn't had heart attacks out of the blue in a bathroom they shouldn't have been using.

As houses go, it's unremarkable. Red brick. Two up, two down. A tarmac drive with a garage. A scruffy patch of lawn and fairy lights in the front window. Upstairs, one bedroom has pink curtains. Emma's room, I suppose.

I waited a while before knocking, and I'm disappointed when the front door opens. She's prettier than I expected. And so young.

'Can I help you?'

She steps back and holds a hand across her face as if that might protect either of us.

'I was with Robert,' I say.

She looks around as if he might somehow appear. And then, she works it all out.

'Did he suffer?' she says in a voice that suggests tears might be close. 'Was there anything you could have done?'

I manage a smile. It's probably what she wants right now.

'I called the ambulance.'

She stumbles and grabs onto the door frame.

'Do you want ... you should come inside. It's cold.'

I hold out an envelope. 'This is for you and little Emma.'

She says nothing, and I can't see the point in hanging around and trying to explain who I am or why I came into her life.

I'm not sure I can explain it all. Not really.

I can't afford another taxi home, so I walk. It's chilly but not freezing. It never is gets that cold at Christmas these days.

I reach the shops on the corner of my road. Someone has draped a string of bulbs over doorways, with every third or fourth one broken or blown. From the always-open Miracle Market, a tinny speaker plays carols...

'Florence,' says the young guy behind the counter. 'What are you doing out and about on Christmas Day? Up to no good, I bet.'

His name is Mick, and I've always found him very handsome. He has dark eyes, freckles, and under his baggy jumper, a body that's seen time in a gym.

I smile and nod at the shuttered cigarette cupboard.

'A filthy habit,' I say. 'But what's life if you can't take a few chances?'

As I pay, our eyes meet.

'Not with your family this year?' he says.

I shake my head. 'Lockdown.'

He nods. 'Same here.'

I'm about to leave the shop when an idea forms.

'Say no if you're not up for it,' I say. 'But you don't fancy earning a few quid doing some odd jobs, do you?'

We Collide

'You know your lines?' Judy says, and Ryan nods. 'You're sure this isn't too weird?'

'It's just weird enough.'

Her hand hesitates on the car door.

'You're right. It's madness. I'll drop you at the bus station.'

'A deal is a deal. And you promised award-winning sausage rolls.'

The girl who stopped to pick him up at Gordano motorway services made a deal. In exchange for a lift to the Cornish coast, Ryan was to meet her parents and pretend to be a loving partner.

'I promise you won't need to stay longer than an hour,' Judy says.

A woman he takes to be her mother waves from the front door of a stone cottage.

'Do you want to run through our history again?' he says. 'Just to be on the safe side.'

Judy's lips don't move. 'Where did we meet?'

'At a book club.'

'What's your job?'

'I'm a therapist.'

'Do we want children?'

'Not at this point.'

She breathes deep. Is this such a good idea? 'If Mum talks wedding favours, change the subject.'

Up close, Ryan finds himself taken by how much Judy looks like her mother. Blonde hair and the same pale blue eyes shot through with the same calm.

'So this is Trevor?' She leans in for a kiss. 'We've heard so much about you.'

Judy's face says just go with it.

'All good, I hope,' he says.

'Any man who can put up with my daughter deserves a medal.' She chuckles. 'But seriously, I'm astonished you got away at this time of year. Isn't there an enormous need for people like you?'

'Trevor picks his hours,' Judy says. 'That's the advantage of being your own boss.'

After taking off their shoes, they're shown into the living room, where an open fire burns under a shelf of framed photographs.

'So far, so good,' he whispers when Judy's mother goes to make tea. 'Should we hold hands or something?'

A little white dog pads into the room, teeth bared at the sight of a stranger. Judy reaches down to rub his head.

'Ted won't hurt a soul.'

Someone makes their way down creaking stairs. She straightens and forces a smile. 'Time to meet your future father-in-law. He won't bite either.'

Michael Browning announces himself, shares a firm handshake, then moves to warm himself in front of the fire.

'So you've finally found someone,' he says. 'We'd given up hope.'

Ryan feels sorry for how easily Judy plays along, how she agrees she struck lucky to land a living, breathing man. One good enough to meet the parents.

'I always thought we'd be lumbered with her,' Michael says with a wink. 'If you want to get out, this is your chance.'

'Why would I want to get out?' Ryan says, and his fake fiancé shifts awkwardly.

Michael stares in confused wonder.

'I'd best get more logs,' he says. 'The weather might turn.'

'Did I say something wrong?' Ryan asks as the patio doors close.

Judy pats his hand. 'Dad's not used to people answering back. He used to be a bank manager.'

Tea arrives, and Ryan says thank you before realising he doesn't yet know Judy's mother's name.

'Susan,' she says, as if reading his mind. 'None of that Mrs Gerald nonsense. We're Michael and Susan to you.' She grins at her daughter. 'Or Mumbie and Popsie, perhaps?'

'They're watching us,' Judy says as they wander by a shallow stream that borders the garden. 'Follow me.'

She leads the way between trees and into a spot hidden from view.

'Are you OK?' Ryan says.

She reaches into her pocket for a pack of cigarettes and offers him one. He waves it away. Judy lights up, inhales deeply, and closes her eyes. 'This got out of hand fast.'

'Do they think we're engaged?'

'I told them I was expecting Trevor to pop the question. They've kind of assumed.'

'Where's the ring?'

'I might have said you—Trevor—wanted me to have his grandmother's ring, but it needed to be adjusted.'

'Does Trevor exist?'

She studies his face, then shakes her head. 'I was sick of them asking when I planned to settle down and churn out grandkids. I figured if they thought there was somebody in my life, they might give it a rest.'

'Surely, at some point, they'd want to meet him?'

'It wasn't my proudest moment.'

He leans against a tree. 'What if we come clean and explain everything? They'll see the funny side, surely?'

Judy pales. 'Promise me you won't do that.'

'The thing is,' he says, trying to work out how best to land his next request, 'my brother and his wife are expecting me. I'm concerned that if I don't turn up soon, they'll call the police?'

'Are you a wanted man?'

'People worry. You know what it's like these days. Big Brother is everywhere. They'll trace me to the motorway services, and I bet there's CCTV of your car picking me up. What will Mumbie and Popsie say if six men in uniform kick down the front door to rescue me from a kidnapper?'

She considers this. 'Call your brother, explain what's happened.'

'I left my mobile inside.'

Judy looks briefly annoyed and hands him her phone.

Ryan's brother asks all the right questions. Is this Judy person stable? Is he safe? Is she holding a gun to his head as they speak?

'I'm fine,' Ryan says. 'It's a situation that went a weird way. She's totally cool. I'd go so far as to say she's nice. I want to help her.'

Judy's face colours, and she turns away. Had they met in any other way, who knows what might have transpired? He's handsome in a rugged way. She could do something about his hair. Kit the guy in decent basics and he'd pass for boyfriend material. And anybody willing to help someone so obviously unstable has to be worth a second glance.

Ryan ends his call and turns to Judy. 'Am I staying the night?'

She shrugs. 'We could pretend, and when everyone's asleep, you sneak off, and I'll say you had an emergency to deal with.'

'Fine by me. When do I get to see the sausage rolls?'

So, now he's staying the night, Judy thinks. This doesn't have to be odd. There's a spare duvet in the hall cupboard. It's not like Mum and Dad will check on sleeping arrangements.

'Do you have pyjamas?' she says as they hold awkward hands and walk back towards the house.

'I sleep in the nip.'

'Not tonight, champ,' she says, and he laughs.

Judy wonders what that might look like, then thinks of something else entirely. Older men playing bowls. Dogs running through long grass. The weird noise Trevor used to make when he snored. Like someone breathing their last. If only she'd realised in time.

Christmas Eve dinner turns out to be an epic affair. Drinks are served with the promised sausage rolls. Six courses follow, each more impressive than the last. The meal ends with brandy and home-baked biscuits.

'You're a wonderful cook, Susan,' Ryan says, hoping his words don't slur.

Susan fans herself. 'One does what one can.'

'I suppose we're on washing-up duty,' Michael says with a glance in Ryan's direction.

There's an awkward silence that Judy punctures. 'There is a dishwasher. Dad probably wants to check your intentions towards me are honourable.'

Ryan helps carry plates to the kitchen and is about to return for more when Michael corners him.

'My daughter is right. I engineered things to chat about your intentions towards her. I want to be sure Judy's in safe hands.'

'She is.'

'And you know her history?'

Ryan stiffens. How can someone so sorted and sane, so beautiful and easy to talk to, have a history?

'Because not every man wants to take on such a handful.'

Michael reaches into a drawer and produces two cigars. 'Follow me, young man. We'll talk in the conservatory.'

Ryan has never smoked a cigar. He knows not to inhale; that's about it.

Michael holds court. 'My daughter isn't an easy person to love. I'm sure you've discovered that for yourself. Three years is impressive, though. Most of her suitors take flight after three months.'

'Well, you know how it is. Every old sock finds an old shoe.'

Michael studies him. 'That's a strange way to put it, but I suppose I understand. When Judith's sister... did what she did... we all found it hard to cope. I won't pretend I understood. I probably didn't help. I drank a lot. It's what people like me do. We blot out feelings.'

A line has been crossed.

'My daughter still blames herself. It's the reason for the... you know what.'

Ryan weighs his response. Nod? Smile? Neither feels right.

Michael wipes mist from the enormous windows and stares at the frost-kissed lawn. 'It's rather cheering to know she's found someone like you. Someone in the profession, so to speak.'

'The profession?'

'You deal with fruit loops and nutters all the time, surely?'

Ryan's stomach knots. 'I don't think that's a helpful way to talk about mental illness.'

'Mental?' Michael sounds out the word. 'Is that what we call them these days?'

Ryan's cigar has gone out. He looks for an ashtray.

'Had you ever met my daughter before today?'

A flash of white in the garden. Michael hauls open the door. 'Ted! Come here, boy. You shouldn't be outside. The bloody foxes will have you.'

Judy appears, eyes meeting Ryan's. What did her father say?

'Mum says your programme is on.'

'Tell her she needs to keep an eye on the bloody dog,' Michael mutters. 'We're on our way.'

'What did Dad want to talk about?' Judy asks later, when every other head in the house has given in to sleep. Ryan is wrapped in the spare duvet on her bedroom floor.

'I think he wanted to be sure I had good intentions.'

'Did he mention Amelia?'

'Who?'

'My sister.'

A shiver creeps up his spine. 'Ted interrupted us.'

Judy sighs and stares at the ceiling. 'So that's a yes?'

'It's none of my business.'

'Amelia drowned in the stream at the bottom of the garden. She was three. I was still a baby.'

'I'm sorry. That must have been awful for everyone.'

'I was crying, and Mum was doing her best to comfort me. My sister slipped. They've said enough times they don't blame me, but...'

Ryan sits up. 'How old were you?'

'Four months.'

'Four-month-old babies cry. It's what they do.'

'He still blames me.'

'I'm not sure he does. He seemed more bothered about making sure I wasn't trying to pull the wool over your eyes. He cares, Judy. He really does.'

'Their eyes lit up when I said you were a psychotherapist. They think you're trying to fix me.'

The air stills.

'Do you need fixing?' he says.

Judy turns to face him, propping her head on her hand. 'I think everybody does.'

They lie in silence. Then she lifts the edge of her duvet. 'You're frozen down there. I keep asking them to leave the central heating on at night, but Dad refuses.'

'I'm fine. Anyway, I need to make my escape soon.'

When Ryan's eyes next open, the only light in the room comes from a digital alarm clock.

It's 4 a.m.

He never meant to sleep.

'Judy,' he whispers.

No reply.

'Judy, are you awake?'

He listens for her breathing. Nothing.

'Judy.' Louder now.

He rests a hand where she should be. Cold sheets.

She's gone.

He picks his way down creaking stairs, tiptoes past Ted's basket, checks the sitting room, dining room, study. One patio door is ajar.

He steps into the brittle cold, follows the lawn's silvered edge, and finds the path to the stream.

'Judy,' he whispers. 'Are you down here?'

'Ryan. This way.'

She sits on the bank, wrapped in a jacket, feet bare.

'Is this to do with what you told me earlier?' he says.

'Sort of.'

Silence settles hard.

'It's freezing,' he says at last. 'We should go back inside.'

She nods and lets him take her hand.

Their footprints trail in the frost.

The kettle boils. Ryan makes tea.

'Have you ever tried to get help for how they make you feel?' he says. Judy cocks her head. 'They probably don't blame you at all.'

She smiles to herself. This man who owes her nothing wants to help. As he pours water into a white teapot, she dares herself to speak.

'Take me with you.'

'Where?'

'To Normalland. To meet your brother and his wife. Where do they live, anyway?'

'Near Truro. I was going to see if I could talk you into dropping me somewhere near a bus.'

'It's Christmas tomorrow. They won't be running.'

Upstairs, a toilet flushes. Judy signals for quiet. When a bedroom door closes, she speaks again.

'I love them, but they can't love me back. Most of the time, it's fine. We rattle by in our separate lives. Me up in Liverpool. Them down here. Phone calls, cards, money in my bank account for my birthday. But Christmas is different. We collide.'

'They seem happy to have you here.'

'We're playing our allocated roles, Ryan. I'm the submissive nutcase daughter. They're the loving parents who never mention the past.' She takes his hand. 'When I first asked you if you'd pretend to be my partner, what did you say?'

'Was it something to do with the central locking? Did I ask to be set free?'

'You asked if I'd return the favour and convince your brother you're not a total waste of space who can't land a bird.'

'Did I say "bird"?'

She nods. 'I'm afraid you did.'

'Don't judge me. I was nervous.'

'So what do you think?' She turns her smile up full. 'That's if you're not ashamed to be seen with me.'

'I'm not sure I'd want to impose my nephews on anyone. They're at the stage where they find farting hilarious.'

'It sounds perfect,' she says. 'Just for once, I'd like to spend Christmas with people who fart openly.'

Ryan unloads carefully wrapped gifts from the boot of Judy's car. Together, they arrange them under the tree. Judy sits at the kitchen table and writes a note.

'It's better this way,' she says. 'They're too polite to ask me not to come. I'm too weak to suggest staying away.'

Outside, the sky glows pink. Morning comes soon.

'You think we'll tell the grandkids this is how we met?' she says.

Ryan isn't sure he heard right. 'Are you suggesting?'

Judy crosses the room.

Her head rests on his shoulder.

Five Gold Rings

Estate agents suck. They're happy to wax lyrical about double glazing, wet rooms, and still-under-guarantee boilers. The little lad in a shiny suit who showed us around boasted of how the street had a genuine community feel.

Turns out that was a nice way of calling the neighbours insufferable.

'People pay extra to be part of a ready-made social circle,' he said. 'And you're near the park.'

That we had to see the place three times before we made an offer should have served as a warning sign. I'm a firm believer that hell is other people. St Nicholas Close was our second choice. We'd set our hearts on a cute terrace near the station. Perfect for my London commute, and Clair could cycle to work.

The horrors of a property chain ended that dream, and desperate to escape my in-laws' spare room, we exchanged contracts and became the proud owners of a tiny house in a narrow Hove street with no vehicle access.

5 St Nicholas Close.

'Have we made the biggest mistake ever?' Clair said as I supervised grumpy removal men. 'Can we return the keys and say we changed our minds?'

I laughed, but if she was having doubts, I was having kittens.

Until that morning, I hadn't truly clocked the cashmere-clad, dead-eyed drones who drifted around like Boden catalogue models.

'So, you're moving in?' said a smooth-faced woman as she pushed a complex buggy with huge rubber wheels. 'We'll be neighbours.'

She was blonde and pretty.

Clair interrupted. 'You must come by for coffee after we get everything settled. I'm Martin's wife.'

I left them to chat and disappeared to give the removal guys a hand.

'You never said it was traffic-free,' the gaffer said as he rolled a cigarette. 'We charge for the extra hours.'

'Of course,' I said, trying to act like one of the lads.

My face ached from smiling. My spirits were low. The ache in my belly suggested an ulcer.

'She's called Molly,' Clair said later. 'That pretty woman with the buggy. And her daughter is Persephone.'

'How have we ended up in a street where people call their kids Persephone?'

'Her husband is called Jeremiah. She wittered on about matcha tea. I was out of my depth.'

'Which number does she live in?'

'Number eleven, I think. The one with plantation blinds. I mentioned that we were getting takeaway tonight, and she looked at me like I'd suggested we kept coal in the bath.'

'They can't all be like that,' I said. 'Surely.'

'I told her it was that or Pot Noodle, and she was outraged.'

I love Clair. We get each other. Neither of us ever planned to end up in Hove. We saw ourselves as London people and rented a funky flat in Brixton. We always thought we'd buy something similar. Until every estate agent laughed us out of town. Brighton seemed a fair compromise, given Clair already worked there. Hove became a decent third choice.

'What kind of takeaway are we getting?' I said as we huddled on the sofa that first night.

'I found this pizza leaflet. It's ridiculously expensive, and they only use organic everything. You order, I'm going to get a bath.'

We'd grown used to pizza from a tiny Italian place on the corner of our old street. I wasn't ready for more change, but the guy who took my order was very friendly. Right until I gave him our new address.

'St Nicholas Close?'

'Yeah, you know it?'

'Are you new?'

'Just moved in.'

'Thought so.'

'So… how long for the pizza?'

'I'll do it this once, but you need to meet my delivery boy by the bollards.'

He explained that St Nicholas Close was a pizza no-go zone. Not because his delivery guys feared for their lives. God knows it was hardly the Wild West. His beef lay with our neighbours. Or rather, the couple at number three: Geoffrey and Maude. Apparently, they disapproved.

'What if they see me?' I said as I pulled on my coat. 'We'll become social pariahs.'

Clair vanished into the front room and returned with a duffel bag.

'Use this.'

A week later, it was Halloween. At the end of the close, Colin and Guy from the big house threw a party.

Fancy dress compulsory.

'We'll meet all the neighbours in one go,' Clair said. 'That's a good thing, right?'

We dressed in black, painted our faces white, and drew stitches on our arms in eyebrow pencil. If only we'd known.

Everyone else had used stylists to transform into characters from hit horror movies. Colin and Guy's house offered apple bobbing, a candyfloss stall, and a professional dancer who taught kids how to moonwalk.

We lasted an hour. I ended up in the kitchen with a blousy woman called Elouise.

'So you're new in at number five?' she said and honked with laughter. 'It makes you sound like something by Abba.'

Elouise found her joke hilarious, as did her husband, Digsby, and their best friends, Theo and Ralph. They treated everyone to a replay. I laughed, too. Every time. It seemed the right thing to do.

And then Geoffrey from number three appeared.

Everyone shut up as he walked down the line, nodding like the Queen meeting hopeful performers after a bum-challenging three-hour Royal Variety Show.

'I suppose you're new,' he said when he got to me. 'You'll know better next time.'

I forced a smile.

'Ignore him,' Elouise said afterwards. 'We all think he's a horror.'

She laughed again. So did Digsby, Theo, and Ralph.

For Bonfire Night, St Nicholas Close turned into a war zone.

Geoffrey and Maude laid on a firework display set to Verdi's *Requiem*. The Chinese family opposite gave everyone paper lanterns, and we gathered on the edge of the park and released them.

It all felt terribly spiritual.

'Make a wish, Martin,' Clair whispered.

'I wish we'd never seen that bloody house.'

'Me too.'

We held each other close as Elouise laughed and took photos.

When a silver envelope with curly-swirly writing landed on the doormat, I thought it early for cards.

Someone addressed it to The Family at Number Five.

I tossed it on the side and thought nothing more of it. Christmas cards are Clair's domain. She buys an enormous box from John Lewis, and we production-line them the evening before the last post.

When I got home from work, she was in a state.

'Why didn't you call me, Martin?'

'About what?'

She waved the envelope in my face. 'I can't compete with these people. It's too much.'

'You're not making sense. Take a deep breath and tell me what's happened.'

Clair showed me the letter. From the St Nicholas Close Residents' Association. Signed by Geoffrey and Maude.

It's that time of the year again, when we get to celebrate our namesake.

Yes, it's ADVENT CALENDAR MONTH.

It probably doesn't take a genius to work out you'll wow us with window number five!!!

Please make sure you close all downstairs curtains on the last day of November and only open them at dawn on the fifth day of December.

There's a unique prize for the best display.

'You always complain nobody does much for Christmas,' I said. 'And it's not like they're expecting us to throw a house party.'

Clair looked set to explode.

'You know what Geoffrey is like. He's ultra-competitive. And when did Advent have anything to do with St Nicholas? Whatever happened to the baby Jesus?'

'We could pretend we never saw the letter. He'll let us off. We're new.'

'It was hand-delivered.'

She sat at the kitchen table and fired up her laptop.

'What can we do? Obviously not a stable. That's for the guys at number 25.'

'Five gold rings,' I said, and her hopeful face encouraged detail.

'I'll buy five rubber rings from the pound shop and spray them gold. If we hang them in the window, Bob's your uncle.'

Clair's expression changed. She turned her laptop for me to see.

'This is hardcore. Look at what the couple at number nine did last year.'

It was a photo of a window that offered views of what looked like an enchanted forest. White paper trees lined a faux-frosty lane. Red-breasted robins floated above a jolly snowman.

'That's Oxford Street-standard,' I said, and she nodded. 'Five rubber rings from the pound shop won't cut it.'

We opened wine to brainstorm ideas.

'What else comes in fives?' she said.

'Fingers?'

'Yeah, right, so we'll put a severed hand in the front window. Talk sense, Martin.'

'The Jackson Five.'

'Half of them are dead.'

'There were five *Rocky* movies... or did they stop at four?'

As she opened a second bottle, I called interior designers. Three politely told me to get stuffed. A fourth—someone called Lavinia—promised to come by at the weekend to discuss concepts. She made it sound pricey.

'How much is this going to cost?' I said.

She laughed. 'It will cost you more if you don't use me. I did Sue-Lin's window last year. It was a triumph. She's due to call me any day now for a repeat performance.'

Clair insisted we pay a deposit. Why leave anything to chance?

The best thing about Thursdays is that I get to work from home, which means blasting loud music and staying in pyjamas past lunch.

The doorbell rang at eleven.

A guy in a brown uniform looked me up and down, unimpressed. I wondered if a by-law stated that St Nicholas Close people should be appropriately attired when answering front doors.

'There's no answer at number three,' he said. 'So, if you wouldn't mind signing here.'

'Signing for what?'

'Their delivery.'

'Can't you leave a card?'

'I can hardly take them back.'

'Why not?'

'Livestock, mate. We're not set up for it.'

Intrigued, I followed him down the close. In the back of his van sat three wooden crates, and in each, a chicken.

'I suppose I could take them in,' I said. 'But make sure number three knows I've got them.'

A little after four, the doorbell rang again.

It was Geoffrey, and he didn't look happy.

'Have you told anyone?' he said before I got to speak.

'Told anyone what?'

'About the bloody hens.'

'Ah, right,' I said. 'You've come to pick up your delivery.'

'So... have you told anyone?'

'Have I told anyone you were out when someone tried to deliver three chickens?'

'Three French hens,' he said with a sour note of irritation. 'For the window.'

He looked at me like it should have been obvious.

'How's that going to work?' I said. 'Won't they make a mess?'

'We're transforming the space. Maude knows an up-and-coming visual artist with a studio in Shoreditch. He's coming to paint a gigantic mural of the *Mona Lisa* on the back wall. We're scattering genuine French straw if I can get it through DEFRA.'

'It sounds... lovely.'

'Right, so have you told anyone?'

'Well... no. Apart from Clair.'

'Your wife?'

'We're not married.'

He looked vaguely annoyed. 'Mum's the word?'

I wanted him to go, though obviously not before he agreed to relieve me of chickens.

'So, where are they?' he said.

I showed him through to the back garden. He peered first at the birds, and then at me.

'What the buggery bollocks are these?'

'Three French hens?'

'They're Appenzeller Spitzhauben. What were you thinking of, man? Why did you accept them?'

'Because I had no idea their provenance mattered.'

'Of course it bloody matters. This isn't good enough. I must phone the supplier right away. I specifically said Bresse Gauloise.'

He stormed back through our house, trailing garden mud across beige carpets.

'Shall I give you a hand with them?' I called after him, but he was away. Most likely to phone whoever sent the non-French hens. Anyone else might use a mobile. He struck me as the landline sort.

Half an hour later, I steeled myself to knock on his door, and when he answered, Geoffrey acted surprised.

'Brian, isn't it?'

'Martin. About the chickens.'

He laughed. 'Yes, what a palaver. They're collecting them on Thursday.'

He tried to shut the door.

'Shall I give you a hand with them?' Geoffrey's eyes

narrowed. 'I mean, I could probably manage on my own, but...'

'Right you are. I dare say they'll come about the same time. You never can tell, though, with delivery drivers. Best you stay in all day.'

The door closed.

I knocked again.

'Did you forget something, old chap?'

'Your chickens...'

'They'll be fine with water and stale bread. It's only until Thursday.'

'Yes, so shall I bring them round?'

'Why would you do that? They're not what I ordered.'

'Yes, but by that logic, they're also not what I ordered.'

'But I've given the delivery man your address now. It will only confuse matters if I change things. Best we leave things as they are, eh?'

He patted my arm and shut the door again.

'Three French hens?' Clair said.

'Yeah, but they're actually Swiss. I looked it up online. Apparently, the breed has a reputation for being flighty— easily calmed with gentle handling.'

'So I can't wring their necks and stuff them with Paxo?'

'I promised Geoffrey we'd keep them safe.'

'Yeah,' Clair said. 'You would.'

It was only when I revealed details of Geoffrey's *Mona Lisa*-meets-French-country-estate tableau that her eyes widened.

'Phone Lavinia, see if she can come sooner.'

I did as she said, and when Lavinia answered, she sounded distant.

'I've been meaning to call. Bad news, I'm afraid. Sue-

Lin has insisted I help her again, and she was such an absolute darling last year that I had to say yes.'

'But you promised.'

'Gosh, I'm sorry, darling. If I could help, you know I would, but Sue-Lin has insisted on exclusivity. Obviously, I'll return the deposit less my agreed handling fee.'

I decided not to tell Clair. She was in the kitchen shredding a head of lettuce; it didn't feel like the right moment.

The next morning, as we headed out to work, she cornered me. 'When is that designer woman coming?'

'She promised to call later today.'

'We need to get a move on, Martin. I saw a theatrical supplies van outside number two yesterday. It's less than three weeks until we have to reveal our window.'

My stomach ached with guilt.

'I'll call her,' I said. 'See if she can come tonight.'

On the way home, I got flowers, and called into Waitrose to buy a meal deal. And wine. Three bottles. That way, even if Clair locked herself in the bathroom to sob, I'd have standby Merlot.

When she walked through the front door, I greeted her with a glass of red and a big smile.

'What did you break?' she said.

'Nothing, but hurry upstairs. I ran you a bath. Dinner will be ready in half an hour.'

She was onto me at once. 'Lavinia isn't coming, is she?'

I shook my head.

I'd expected her to explode or at the least curl up in a furious ball and cry. Instead, she handed me her coat.

'Something smells lovely,' she said. 'Shall we eat it on trays in front of the telly?'

Against all odds, we had the most wonderful evening,

watching TV, chatting about our days, and drinking too much wine. She never brought up the window once.

I lay in bed, terrified.

❄

The first day of December dawned, and we'd not agreed on a theme. Clair remained in tense denial.

'What are we doing about the window?' I said when the fear took hold.

'Who cares?'

'We can't not do one. Even if we paint a huge number five and stick it out front, we have to do something.'

Raised voices drifted from the street. We dived into the front room to peer through a gap in the curtains. It was Angela from number one and the guys from number 25.

'You can't do that,' Colin squared up to Angela. 'It's not fair.'

'Where is it written?'

'Everyone knows we reveal the Nativity scene on the 25th. It's our gig. We always do it.'

'So just this once, why not switch things around? You've got three weeks to come up with something.'

'We've already paid five grand to an animatronics company for an Angel Gabriel.'

Clair nudged me. 'And you wanted to spend a fiver at the pound shop.'

Other neighbours emerged to witness the fight.

Geoffrey waded in.

'Angela,' he said. 'You know the rules. Guy and Colin always get the stable.'

'That's not fair.'

'It's entirely fair. What if we all opted for stables? Where would that leave the world?'

'Why does it matter?'

'It's heresy, Angela. You can't have Jesus born on the first day of Christmas. What's wrong with a partridge in a pear tree?'

'Jesus,' she said. 'The Twelve Days of Christmas. What sort of moron would do that?'

Clair nudged again, and this time she looked smug.

The argument dragged on for a good half-hour until Guy became inconsolable and Colin threatened legal action.

'Can we double our offer to Lavinia?' I said. 'I'm sure she'd take pity on us if we maxed out all our credit cards.'

Clair shook her head and took hold of my hand.

'This was supposed to be a surprise...'

Before we wheeled our cases through the front door, we dragged the TV into the front room, tuned it to Channel 5 and opened the curtains.

'It's enough,' Clair said simply. 'The taxi will be waiting.'

Geoffrey left an angry message on my phone.

We sipped cocktails in the airport lounge and listened.

'An absolute disgrace,' he ranted. 'Bounders and cads. Unworthy.'

'I don't think I'll be getting my Tupperware back,' Clair said, and we both laughed.

Three blissful weeks stretched ahead of us. Time for ourselves in the sun. Away from the madness. We'd be back on Boxing Day. The 26th. The day after it all ends.

'They say it will be twenty-three degrees today,' Clair said and topped up her glass with freshly squeezed orange juice.

I reached for coffee. 'Shall we stick to the pool?'

Geoffrey's angry tirades continued. Each day, he issued fresh insults.

Colin and Guy appeared.

'We're all heading into town this evening for dinner. Are you joining us?'

Across the terrace, Sue-Lin's kids played tag. Molly failed to tempt Persephone away from the churro stand with fresh fruit. Elouise set up her easel to paint.

I reached for Clair's hand. 'Who needs five gold rings?'

A solitaire sparkled on her ring finger.

Lasagne For One

Hate nobody. Hate is a negative emotion. Make your enemy your friend. Even when your enemy is your boss. Even when that woman is Marjorie: a woman able to turn any conversation toxic with a well-timed put-down or withering stare.

Livvy chants mindful mantras as Marjorie outlines the perfect storm of low reader numbers and declining advertising revenue. Polar Magazine—once the leader of the glossy style pack—was struggling. Last week, they had people in from head office, and if the rumour mill is right, a big announcement is due.

'We need to move mountains, people,' Marjorie says, and across the table, New Boy Joseph nods enthusiastically.

Lick-arse.

Try as she might, Livvy can't bring herself to feel anything but disdain for their new sports editor. Since when did a women's style mag need a sports editor? All he's contributed so far is a fluff piece.

Six ways Venus Williams stays trim.

Marjorie folds her arms, and her eyes travel down the table.

'It's time for change.'

Livvy's heart hammers. Is this the big announcement? If her boss gets moved aside to some other post in head office, the search starts for Polar's new editor. Everyone knows as deputy she'll get first refusal. As Christmas presents go, it would be perfect. There's so much she can do to win back readers.

'We can no longer ignore digital,' Marjorie says. 'It's insufficient to lift and shift print content to the website. Nobody wants to read long features. The photo spreads lose their edge. Nothing translates.'

The sycophants within near-slapping range nod in agreement.

'Christian Haller is from our digital team.'

A guy with a flannel shirt and hipster beard takes over.

Christian drones through plans for a spin-off website, filled with content re-cut for brief attention spans. 'The Fielding party will be our try-out,' he says.

Livvy glances across the table at Joseph. He's scribbling notes. Surely he can't expect to cover the launch of Sallie Fielding's signature scent. She's a soap star. And fair enough, she's married to a footballer. But aren't they all?

'I'd like to work that,' Joseph says.

Marjorie peers over thin-rimmed glasses. 'I never had you down as gender-fluid.'

'I can talk to Frank Fielding. Get his take on things. Everyone else will want to talk about the fragrance. I'll get you the true backstage drama.'

Acid burns Livvy's throat. The little shite hawk.

'Here's the deal,' Marjorie says. 'I'm teaming you up with Olivia. Both of you file a story. I'll take the best one.'

She points a manicured fingernail in Livvy's direction. 'That's fine with you, isn't it? You enjoy healthy rivalry.'

As Livvy trails the others from the boardroom, Marjorie clears her throat. 'Olivia, darling. Can we have a word?'

'Sure... now?'

'No time like the present. Let's go where nobody can listen in.'

She shivers on a windswept fire escape as Marjorie smokes.

'The Fielding gig,' she says. 'It's not what it seems.'

Livvy finds herself intrigued. 'Tell me more.'

'New York wants me to choose an editor for the new venture. I suggested your name. They want someone new. In their eyes, it's between you and Joseph. Until five minutes ago, I had no notion how to pick.'

'It all comes down to which of us files the strongest story?'

'He's got the right idea, Olivia. Avoid the obvious. Write against type. If you turn in a rehashed press release or blow smoke up Sallie Fielding's bumhole, he'll get the job.'

'Right.'

'Something is going on there. Frank Fielding fills a mean pair of boxer shorts, but he's as dumb as a box of hair. I've been getting divorce vibes for months.'

'You want me to dig into their private lives?'

'This is where you have the edge. Sallie's a girl's girl. Suck up. Find out what's making her tick. Get me a scoop.'

'Is Joseph in on this?'

Marjorie flicks her cigarette butt over the office balcony, not caring that the street below bustles with Christmas shoppers.

'What do you think?'

Livvy looks up from reading an email to see Joseph perched on the end of her desk, arms folded, his floppy dark fringe covering one eye.

'So, it's you against me?' he says, and pulls what she imagines he thinks is a face that will melt hearts. He most likely spends hours in front of his bathroom mirror getting it just right. Spoiler alert: heart not melting.

'I'd rather not see it as a competition,' she says.

'Did I ever tell you about playing poker with Frank in the Groucho?'

Livvy's heart quickens. 'Did I ever tell you about drinking cocktails with Sallie in Soho?'

It's a lie, but Sallie drinks cocktails in Soho. Livvy drinks cocktails in Soho when she can afford it. Technically, the two things could have happened at the same time.

Joseph winks. 'Game on.'

When he's in the office kitchen laughing with his mates, she types his name into a search engine. Page after page of photos scroll by. In one, he's shirtless. Who'd have guessed a gym-toned body lurked under that ugly, chunky sweater?

She tries again, this time adding Frank Fielding's name.

There they are. Together. Laughing like old mates.

She's officially and royally screwed.

A taxi drops Livvy at the end of the Mall. The police have cordoned off the street, so she's forced to walk the rest of the way in stupidly high heels and a dress created for women whose chief life skill involves standing still and smiling. She picks her way through crowds and flashes

Marjorie's ticket at a security guy who waves her past onto a scuffed red carpet.

The cinema foyer feels magical: decorated for Christmas and rammed with famous faces. Across the way, near a line for the bathroom, she spots Frank Fielding glancing at his watch as if waiting for someone.

Should she say hello and send regards from Marjorie?

Sallie is chatting with friends and looks like the perfect pocket princess—clad in red lace with the fullest, brightest smile. Livvy takes a deep breath. She'll compliment Sallie's outfit and ask who did her hair. The trick is to act like they've met before. Famous people rarely recall faces and hate to be labelled standoffish.

Frank is back and puts his arm around Sallie's middle, pulling her close.

And—shit!—there's Joseph, dressed in a tight blue suit, looking the business and swooping in for one of those weird fist-bump greetings.

Joseph interrupts to shake Frank's hand. Their greeting turns into a happy man-hug. A tray of drinks wafts into view, so she takes a glass, drains it in one, and reaches for two more.

There's a line for the bathroom, and the girl in front is one of the chatty sort.

'I wish I'd worn underwear,' she says with a snort. 'My arse is eating this frock.'

Thanks to three glasses of sickly-sweet sparkling wine, Livvy manages a smile.

'I know you,' the girl with the underwear issue points. 'Were you on *This Morning* the other day? Talking about eyeliner?'

Livvy gets this all the time. There's a television beauty

therapist called Martina, and they do look sort of alike. If you squint. And drink enough sparkling wine.

'I work for *Polar*,' Livvy says, and the girl whistles, impressed. 'My editor reckoned tonight might be a good way to meet Sallie Fielding. Unfortunately, my colleague…'

The girl shrieks. 'You want to meet our Sal?'

'Your Sal?'

'I'm Maisie. Sal's sister. Let me sort myself out, and I'll introduce you.'

Without anyone to impress, Sallie Fielding's shy demeanour and clipped accent turn broad, and she doesn't seem to care who overhears her announcement that the film is a bag of sweaty balls.

'You realise you can't repeat any of this?' her sister says, with a squeeze of Livvy's hand.

'Maisie,' Sallie roars. 'Nobody gives a flying fuck about me. Frank's the star tonight.'

Yeah, right, Livvy thinks. Joseph will turn in some dull piece about sport and boy things and how this action-packed thriller is the absolute bees' knees. Sallie has posed for selfies, suggested they meet up for lunch tomorrow, then leaned in to whisper that her mother-in-law is a bitch. There's talk of a restraining order. And her fairytale marriage might not be all it appears.

'Where is my fucking husband, anyhow?' Sallie says.

Livvy dares a peek at her phone. She's going to email Marjorie and declare herself the winner of this dumb contest. And then her giddy world stops turning. She can hardly believe what she sees. Joseph has already filed his story—a scoop on Frank Fielding's miserable marriage.

After the film ends, the cinema foyer empties fast. Livvy checks her phone, but there's no message from Sallie. No promised time and date for their big chat. She's probably been told about her husband's exclusive.

Fucking Joseph.

There's a long line for taxis. Livvy shivers as she shelters from the rain.

'I owe you thanks,' a voice says, and she turns to see Joseph grinning ear to ear. He holds up his phone to let her read a message from Marjorie.

Excellent work. I knew you'd do it.

'Congratulations.' She forces a smile. It hurts. 'I hope you'll be delighted in your new job.'

He cocks his head to one side. 'Don't tell me you're bitter. Someone with your talent... they'll be beating down your door.'

She forces another smile.

Fuck off, Joseph. Just fuck the fuck off.

He rubs his hands together. 'Jesus, it's cold. I don't suppose you fancy a swift drink?'

Livvy's head already aches from free champagne, but the line for cabs has grown longer. What harm will it do?

'Fine. But you're paying.'

Two very Irish coffees later, Joseph loosens his tie and leans back in a soft leather chair.

'How do you do it, Livvy?'

'How do I do what?'

'You come in day after day, knowing you've nothing much to look forward to, yet you always seem so upbeat.'

'Perky,' she says with a shake of the head. 'That's what Marjorie wrote on my last assessment... It could have been worse.'

He laughs. 'That's what I mean. Like water off a duck's back.'

'I have a dark side.'

Their eyes meet. 'I don't believe you.'

'My mission tonight was to suck up to Sallie and put you out of the running. If I'd filed my story first, I wouldn't have given you a second thought.'

A second round of drinks arrives.

'When did you order these?' she says.

'I told the barman to keep them coming.'

She takes a slug. 'Is there anything about you that isn't naff?'

Conversation dies, and before a third very alcoholic coffee can arrive, Livvy pulls out her phone. 'I'm going to order a taxi.'

'Wise,' he says. 'It's gone midnight. I'd hate you to turn into a pumpkin.'

A recorded voice says she's in a queue. The average wait is thirty minutes.

'One for the road?' Joseph says… she hesitates, then nods.

There's a late-night café near the taxi rank. Ideal to shelter from the rain while you wait for the next cab. It's just the two of them and a guy in a greasy vest staring at a television with the sound down.

'What do you want from life?' Livvy breaks an awkward silence that seems to have settled.

Joseph shrugs. 'A job I'm good at. An easy life. Enough money to retire when I'm forty.'

She can't help but notice something missing from his list. 'What about love?'

He shifts uneasily in his chair, thumb finds the end of his nose, and he glances away—classic nervous body language.

'Love?' he says, as if tasting the word for the first time. 'Everyone says that's for mugs.'

'So there isn't anyone? I thought you were seeing one of the girls from the PR team.'

'It didn't work out. She likes long walks in the woods. I'm more of a stay-at-home and watch someone else in the woods on the telly kinda guy.'

'Got any plans for Christmas?'

'Lasagne, for one. A bucket of red wine.'

It hits Livvy like a speeding train. Her plan sounds identical. Except she'll probably add a family-size trifle. And those weird flavours of crisps you only ever get at Christmas.

Livvy feels like shite. Her head bangs, and she now accepts staying out late with Joseph was a dumb idea. Everyone has found time to stop by his cubicle, shake his hand, and say what a great scoop he scored.

And joy of joys. Here comes Marjorie. Dressed in black and white with her hair up, like Cruella de Vil.

'I'd like to see you both in my office,' she snaps, looking at neither of them. 'In twenty minutes.'

Livvy's stomach rolls. Marjorie has no heart, but even she wouldn't sack someone with eight working hours to go before the Christmas shutdown. Half the office is wearing silly sweaters. Everyone is eating mince pies.

Joseph rolls his chair across the aisle that separates their desks. 'How did that sound to you?'

'Like she wants to ruin my life.'

He spots a Marks & Spencer bag under Livvy's desk. 'You got your Christmas dinner, then?'

She reaches in and produces a festive lasagne. 'Made

with turkey mince. I blame the carol singers near the shopping centre.'

'I got the same,' he says. 'What were we thinking?'

To her immense surprise, Livvy finds she feels sort of
OK about losing to Joseph. He isn't an up-himself tosser,
after all. He's arrogant, for sure. He talks too much about
himself, but scratch the surface and...

He jumps up. 'I'll make tea.'

'There's no milk,' she says, but he's already gone.

Livvy finds him in the kitchen, staring at the kettle,
waiting for it to boil.

'Tell you what,' she says. 'After Marjorie has destroyed
my career, we'll have a drink at the Bell.'

The pub started off rammed, but by six-thirty it's all but
empty. The office crowds have hugged each other goodbye
and jumped into cabs or onto buses. All the nearby shops
have closed. It's depressing.

'That was harsh,' Joseph says for what feels like the
tenth fucking time.

Livvy nods slowly. 'At least we're being paid until
March. I suppose I'll start ringing around contacts in the
new year.'

Marjorie didn't sugar-coat her news. The magazine was
finished. In print, anyway. They were moving 100% online
and buying content from freelancers. The entire editorial
team would lose their jobs in the new year.

Tired of an endless post-mortem, Livvy stretches and
looks around. 'What time do they stop serving in here?'

Joseph glances at his phone, checking the time. 'No

idea, but we need something to lift the mood. I'm going to order the best champagne this shithole sells.'

A cork pops, flies across the bar, and lands in the middle of an over-decorated Christmas tree. A nearby table of fellow misfits musters a half-hearted cheer.

'How much did that cost?' Livvy says. 'You're about to be unemployed.'

'It's my Christmas present to you.'

'Oh, right?' She tries not to show how this throws her. 'But I have to share it with you?'

'I'm out of work, mate. Can't afford one of my own.'

She pours and proposes a toast. 'To single lasagne lovers everywhere.'

Livvy swings an angry arm to restore silence when her alarm clock beeps. It's not like she needs to crawl from her bed early. It's Christmas Day.

Her head aches, and a trail of clothes leads from the hall.

She lies still.

It was fun spending time with Joseph. Despite their thawing relationship, until last night, she still had him down as a twat of the highest order. United in defeat and sharing horror stories of their soon-to-be ex-boss turned him into a genuine friend. She had toyed with inviting him back for coffee until her inner party monster threw in the towel.

Don't, her sensible self said. You'll only end up shagging him.

A taxi dropped her home alone.

The King begins his annual address, and Livvy picks at

her festive lasagne. It's dry, tasteless, and delivers nothing like the tidings of comfort and joy promised by the packaging.

She dares herself to try another handful of 'Turkey-'n'-all-the-Trimmings' crisps.

They still taste like soap powder.

As she scrapes leftovers into the bin, her intercom buzzes.

'This better not be that creep from downstairs complaining I've got the TV on too loud,' she mutters, catching sight of herself in a mirror while rummaging for keys in coat pockets: bird's-nest hair, a face needing industrial-strength moisturiser, and piggy eyes.

'One minute,' she mumbles into the intercom.

'Hurry, it's freezing.'

Livvy's heart leaps. It's Joseph.

What the actual fuck?

In the bathroom, she quickly straightens her hair and swigs mouthwash.

'I'm not sure who looks worse,' Joseph says as she comes back into the living room. 'Did you try your lasagne yet?'

Livvy stops dead. He's got changed from baggy jogging pants into pyjamas. And Garfield slippers.

He shrugs. 'I knew you'd look like hell. It's only fair I let you see me at my worst, too. Let's find a film about families coming together despite overwhelming odds.'

'I planned on watching a six-part documentary about the Nazis,' Livvy says—and regrets it as he reaches for the remote and finds the History Channel.

As luck would have it, Joseph knows how to transform the contents of a single person's kitchen cupboard and fridge into something edible. Wrapped in woollen blankets, they dig forks into cheesy pasta, glued to a Hallmark Christmas movie.

'We should remember this moment when our grand-kids ask,' he says.

'I plan on ostracising our kids so we never get dragged into babysitting duties.'

'Perfect.'

When Livvy leans in closer, he doesn't move.

The kiss, when it happens, seems inevitable.

Twelve hours hence

I've never been what you'd call gifted. Not in the conventional sense, anyway. When other kids were winning rosettes at the school sports day or getting their drawings pinned up in the corridor, I was the one holding everyone's anoraks. 'You're reliable, Dennis,' my mother used to say, as if reliability was something you'd put on your CV under Special Skills. Though I suppose, in a way, that's exactly what I've done.

The thing started eighteen months ago, 23 June, which I remember because it was the day after my fifty-seventh birthday and I'd just finished the last of the birthday Battenberg that Marjorie from next door had brought round. She always brings Battenberg, has done for fifteen years, though I've never much cared for marzipan. Still, you can't say, can you? Not after fifteen years. The time to object has passed. Any adverse comment at this stage would likely result in a query.

I'd gone to bed with what I thought was indigestion from the cake, and woke up knowing that at 11:47 the next morning, the number 42 bus would break down outside the Tesco Metro, causing a minor traffic incident involving a Ford Fiesta and a woman with a wheely basket full of cat food.

This wasn't something I thought might happen. Not even something I thought would almost certainly happen. I knew it would. The best way to put this for you is to call it a prediction. But even that suggests doubt. And that was the thing. I had absolutely no doubt. It was going to happen. In the order I said. With the people I mentioned involved. Right down to the cat food. If pushed, I could tell you the brand.

And yes, I see how this isn't up there with Cassandra or Nostradamus, but still...

At first, I thought I was having some sort of break-down. Men my age do, apparently. Marjorie's husband Keith went funny at fifty-eight and started collecting beer mats, though that might have been more of a lifestyle choice than a medical condition. But when the bus did indeed break down at 11:47 (11:48 actually, but the driver's watch was slow), and the Ford Fiesta did clip the woman's wheely basket, sending tins of Whiskas Supermeat rolling into the road like some sort of feline meals-on-wheels disas-ter, I wasn't in the least bit surprised.

Right then, Dennis, I said to myself. You appear to have developed some sort of talent. A skill.

The rules became apparent fairly quickly.

I had the ability to see exactly twelve hours ahead, no more, no less. It's like having a very specific and ultimately useless telescope that only focuses at one fixed distance. You can see craters on the moon, but that's your lot. And whilst I've nothing specifically against craters, when you've seen one...

The skill meant I knew, beyond any shadow of doubt,

what I'd be having for breakfast the next morning. Because I saw myself eating it when the titles rolled on *Coronation Street*. Two slices of toast, one with marmalade, one with butter. The butter will be too hard and will tear the bread, but I'll eat it anyway because, well, what's the alternative? Not eating it?

You'd think—wouldn't you?—that seeing the future would be useful. Profitable, even. But there are rules. There always are.

The moment I try to look at anything that might constitute personal gain, the vision goes fuzzy, like trying to watch BBC Two during a thunderstorm in 1978. Lottery numbers? Might as well be in Sanskrit. Horse-racing results? Complete blur. Even finding a pound coin on the street—if I'm going to pick it up tomorrow morning, I can't see it tonight. It's as if the universe has installed some sort of cosmic fairness filter, though given the general unfairness of everything else, this strikes me as selective.

Which brings me to today. Christmas Eve. Or rather, tonight, which is showing me tomorrow's Christmas morning, which is really today's Christmas Day, though by the time you're reading this it might be Boxing Day or possibly next March.

Time, I've discovered, is a lot more complicated when you can see round corners.

I'm in my flat—purpose-built, optimistically described as 'deceptively spacious' by the estate agent in 1994, though what it was deceiving anyone about remains a mystery to me. The decorations are up, if you can call them decorations. A string of lights from Poundland, and a small artificial tree that looks less like a Norwegian spruce and more like something harvested from a back garden near Chernobyl. Still, it's festive. Or at least, it's trying to be festive, which at my age amounts to the same thing.

The thing about seeing twelve hours ahead is that it doesn't stop the present from happening. I still have to live through now to get to the then that I've already seen. It's like being forced to watch a film you've already seen the ending of, except you're also in the film, and you can't fast-forward, and the film is your life, and it's not a particularly good film. More like one of those Sunday afternoon made-for-TV things starring someone who used to be in *Casualty*.

I'm making my Christmas Eve dinner—beans on toast. The beans are Heinz because some things matter, and the toast is wholemeal because my doctor says other things matter too, though I'm not convinced he's right about that.

I glance at the clock. Just gone quarter past six. It's been a day or two since I've had one of my visions, but here one comes now.

At 6:17 tomorrow morning, there's going to be a knock at my door.

I don't get knocks at my door on Christmas morning. I don't get knocks at my door on most mornings. The last person to knock without warning was a Jehovah's Witness, and even they seemed to be doing it more out of obligation than conviction. But there it is, clear as day (clearer actually, given that tomorrow will be overcast with a 40% chance of sleet). Three knocks. Tentative. The kind of knocks that suggest someone hoping you won't answer.

I can see myself getting up, pulling on my dressing gown—the one with the coffee stain on the pocket that looks like a map of Norway—and going to the door.

It's Marjorie knocking. She's wearing her good coat and the brooch her mother left her.

But then—and this is the peculiar part—the vision goes fuzzy. Not the profitable-gain fuzzy, but a different kind. Like the future itself is uncertain, which has never happened before. In eighteen months of seeing twelve hours ahead, tomorrow has always been as fixed as yesterday.

But not this. This is... I suppose *fluid* is the best word for it.

One thing I've not yet told you about Marjorie is that we're sort of 'an item'. She's been my neighbour for fifteen years, ever since her husband Keith left her for a woman he met at a model railway exhibition in Doncaster. I'm her toy boy. At least that's what she tells anyone who'll listen. She's seventy-three, wears glasses on a chain around her neck even though she only needs them for reading.

Given her hip and my lumbago, our love isn't a throw-caution-to-the-wind sort of thing. It's more like the love you might have for a comfortable pair of slippers or a favourite mug. The kind of love that notices when you haven't put your bins out and does it for you without waiting to be thanked. The kind of love that's so quiet and undemanding that you can pretend it isn't there at all.

I can't see what happens after she knocks on my door, because of the fuzziness, but I can see her face just before. It's the face of someone who's decided something. After seventy-three years of not quite deciding things, Marjorie has come to a decision.

The strange thing about knowing the future is that it doesn't make you feel powerful. It makes you feel like a train on tracks, heading towards a destination you can see but can't avoid. Free will becomes a philosophical question rather than a practical one. Can I choose not to answer the door tomorrow morning when Marjorie knocks? Theoretically, yes. But I've already seen myself getting up and putting on the dressing gown, so actually, no. Unless the fuzziness means something different.

Unless, for once, tomorrow isn't fixed.

I met my late wife at a bus stop in 1987. Elaine was waiting for the number 19, I was waiting for the number 23, and both of us were pretending to read the timetable while actually stealing glances at each other. She died in 2003, which is a short sentence for a long sadness. Cancer. She would have been seventy-one this year. She would have liked Marjorie, I think. They had the same way of being disappointed by the world, while still expecting better from it.

I should probably mention that I loved my wife. Love her still, in the present tense, because love doesn't really have a past tense, does it? It just has presence and absence. And I should probably also mention that loneliness isn't the same as being alone. Being alone is a state. Loneliness is a condition. And conditions, my doctor keeps telling me, can be treated.

The fuzziness is bothering me. But I know that if I hold my will and wait, there's every chance the mists will clear and I'll be granted a ringside seat at whatever it is that Marjorie needs to say.

I turn on the telly. BBC. They're showing *The Snowman*. Again. Followed by *Mrs Brown's Boys*. I mute the sound.

For some reason, I'm thinking about Marjorie's husband, Keith. The model railway enthusiast. I've always wondered what sort of woman goes to a model railway exhibition. Marjorie insists she saw it coming. That she wasn't in the least bit surprised when he packed a pale blue

Samsonite and took flight. But she must have been, surely. Unless she's got the same superpower as me.

And I'm fairly sure she hasn't.

I sit very still and shut my eyes. This twelve-hours thing comes and goes and I tend to find it best if I clear my head of any other thoughts.

The thing about Marjorie's knock tomorrow is that I should be able to see what I'm going to say when I open the door. But I can't. The fuzziness extends forward from that moment like fog. I can see myself approaching the door, hand on the latch, and then... nothing clear.

Here's what I know about Christmas: it's a day when people do things they wouldn't normally do. They call people they haven't spoken to all year. They eat things that disagree with them—like sprouts or bread sauce—just to keep the peace. They watch films they've seen a dozen times before and pretend to be surprised by the ending. They make an effort, even when effort seems pointless. Especially when effort seems pointless.

I turn in for the night at eleven. Seven and a quarter hours until Marjorie knocks.

I've been thinking about the rules of my condition. The fuzziness around personal gain makes sense, in a cosmic-justice sort of way. But what if the fuzziness around Marjorie's knock is the same thing? What if answering that door, saying whatever I'm going to say (or not say), leads to some kind of gain? Not money or advantage, but something else. Something the universe's cosmic fairness filter hasn't quite decided how to classify.

I don't sleep easily. Never have done. Elaine tried everything. Hot milky drinks. Magnesium tablets. A bedside light that was supposed to emit a calming glow. It ended up in the PDSA shop.

At midnight, I get out of bed and go over to the window. The street is empty. Most people look to have turned in. Hardly any lights are on in the nearby houses and flats. Somewhere in the distance, I hear church bells, calling folk to Midnight Mass.

When I get back into bed, the sheets are cold, the pillow too flat on one side and too plump on the other. Time passes the way it always does—too fast and too slow simultaneously.

At 3 a.m., I'm still awake.

At 4 a.m., I give in and get up to make a pot of tea. Proper tea, not the decaf nonsense my doctor recommends. If I'm going to be awake, I might as well be properly awake.

The kitchen window shows me the same view it's shown me for twenty-three years—the back of another block of flats, wheelie bins, a tree that might be dead or might just be very committed to playing dead. But tonight, there's a light on in one of the windows opposite. Someone else is awake, unable to sleep on Christmas morning. I wonder if they're excited or afraid or both or neither. I wonder if they can see their future too, or if they're blessed with uncertainty.

Five a.m. One hour and seventeen minutes to go. The fuzziness in my future-vision is getting fuzzier, if that's possible. It's like looking through frosted glass at shapes that might be people or might be furniture or might be nothing at all.

At half past five, I shower and shave. Standards matter, my mother used to say. I get dressed. After all, Marjorie will be on her way soon.

At six o'clock, I sit in my chair and wait. Waiting for the future when you've already seen it is a peculiar form of torture. It's like waiting for a bus when you know exactly when it's going to arrive but can't do anything to make it come faster.

Seven minutes to go and my legs are stiff from sitting. My back aches in the place it always aches.

At 6:15, I go into the hall and wait. I could be ready by the door, but that would be strange. I could scare the life out of Marjorie.

Or is that what happens? Is that why it's fuzzy?

I hear footsteps.

She's outside now.

The knock comes.

Three times, exactly as I saw.

Tentative but determined.

I open the door.

And here's where my vision went fuzzy, so I'm as surprised as anyone to see Marjorie standing there in her good coat and her mother's brooch, holding a Christmas pudding. A proper one, from the look of it. The kind with too much suet and not enough brandy, or possibly the other way around.

'I thought,' she says, and then stops. Starts again. 'I thought you might not have a proper Christmas pudding.'

I say nothing.

'And I thought,' she continues, still holding the pudding like it's a small, fruit-filled life preserver, 'that someone should make sure you have a proper Christmas dinner.'

'That would be nice,' I say, and I mean it.

And then the fuzziness clears, and I can see twelve hours ahead again. I can see us in my kitchen at 6:17 p.m., washing up dishes (plural, not singular). I see the Christmas pudding, half-eaten, with Bird's custard. I see Marjorie in my flat, in my chair, asleep with her mouth a little open in a way that would embarrass her if she knew. I see myself covering her with the blanket from the back of the sofa, the one my wife crocheted in 1998 when she was trying to keep her hands busy during the first round of chemo.

But most importantly, I see that tomorrow—the tomorrow that's twelve hours after that tomorrow—the fuzziness is back. Not around Marjorie this time, but around everything. The future, for the first time in eighteen months, is uncertain. Unclear. Unwritten.

'Would you like to come in?' I say, though I already know the answer because I can see her nodding twelve hours from now, when I ask her the same question again tomorrow.

'I would,' she says. 'I really would.'

She steps inside, and I close the door on the certainty of knowing what comes next. For the first time since 23 June, eighteen months ago, I'm not sure what's going to happen in twelve hours' time.

It's terrifying.

But it's also wonderful.

It's like being normal again, but better, because now I know what a gift uncertainty is.

The fuzziness extends forward now like a gift—undefined hours and uncertain days, decisions not yet made, conversations not yet had. I realise that my useless superpower was never really about seeing the future. It was about learning to appreciate the present, the actual now, the moment when Marjorie adjusts her glasses on their chain and looks at me with eyes that have seen seventy-three years of disappointments and are still capable of hope.

'Dennis,' she says, 'I should probably mention that I don't actually like Christmas pudding.'

'Neither do I,' I admit.

'But we'll eat it anyway?'

'Of course,' I say. 'It's Christmas.'

And for the first time in eighteen months, I have no idea what's going to happen next. And it's the best Christmas present I could have asked for—a future I can't see, arriving one uncertain minute at a time, with Marjorie beside me, both of us pretending to like Christmas pudding while actually, quietly, without making a fuss about it, learning to like each other.

Fine and Dry

The warmest November day on record. That's what the weather presenter promised. And to be fair, it isn't cold. But as I sit on a bench eating my Pret A Manger Christmas dinner sandwich, I wonder if there might be more to life. A guy walks past dressed as Santa, ringing his bell and yo-ho-hoing. Tesco is still selling off Halloween pumpkins, but Christmas is in the air, and I'm determined to enjoy it this year.

Twelve months ago, I woke in Mum and Dad's spare room with my head still sore from drinking mulled wine on the train. I'd tried to get into the mood with a Spotify playlist, but three songs in, I ditched Mariah Carey for Leonard Cohen. The freezing-cold train stopped in every siding as a cheerful driver delivered jolly loudspeaker asides about how he hoped to get everyone home in time for the new year.

'We're all going to Gran's house,' Mum said when she called. 'She's too poorly to travel.'

'Gran, who lives in the middle of nowhere?'

'She's got six bedrooms. It'll be fun.'

'The nearest pub is five miles away.'

'Josie is bringing Michaela and Darcey. Your Auntie Pat said she's coming.'

Auntie Pat is someone Mum used to work with. She's not related.

'It doesn't sound like fun,' I said.

'Bring a friend.'

'There's nobody I hate enough.'

'Well, that's not my problem, is it? I've told her you're coming. She'll have knitted something.'

Gran knits bobble hats. It's a nice enough idea, but her eyesight is shot, and they're more bobble than hat.

'Your sister is putting in an appearance.'

Any mention of Justine strikes terror into my heart.

'What? Why?'

'She's out of rehab.'

My heart sinks further. 'Does that mean...'

'No drink, Laura. It's a dry Christmas.'

Gran greets me with a miserable nod. 'I worried you might not show up. You've drawn the short straw bed-wise. You're in with me.'

I try for a smile, but she sees right through it.

'Nobody told me your sister was coming, either.'

'We'll have fun.'

She leans in to whisper. 'I presume you're smuggling vodka?'

My face flushes.

'Good,' she says. 'I've hidden two bottles of gin in my wardrobe. We'll need something to keep us sane.'

My sister is a lovely person, really. Charming and fun to be around. She's impossible to truly hate, but Mum and Dad regard it as their duty to keep her away from the jar. If anyone so much as mentions drink, they're shot down.

'Is Justine here already?' I say.

'She's in the kitchen making cupcakes.' Gran rolls her eyes. 'As if anyone wants a fecking cupcake.'

I follow her down the dark and narrow hall.

'Laura.' Justine's face lights up. 'I was thinking you weren't coming.'

I let her hug me hello. She looks well, if skinny. The tired bags around her eyes have shrunk, and her smile seems genuine.

'How long has it been now?' I say.

'Sixteen days.'

'Reckon you'll make it to twenty?'

She grimaces. 'Depends on the next twenty-four hours. I assume you've got your own supplies?'

'Of course.'

'If I come knocking...'

'I'll tell you to get the feck away,' I say, and she hugs me again.

Mum and Dad linger down the far end of the garden, and Gran mutters something about them acting like Lord and Lady Muck. Justine taps the window. I wave. Mum smiles.

They traipse in and take off their boots.

'I forget how peaceful it is around here, Diana,' Dad says. 'You're so lucky.'

Gran nods. 'I still wouldn't mind a Tesco Express.'

Mum kisses me hello. 'We're going to gather in the drawing room and sing carols when the sun goes down.'

Justine and I exchange looks. When did Gran have a drawing room?

I lie on the bed and stare at my phone. I shouldn't have called him. But with three days of family stretched before me, what choice did I have? Mum will rage. Dad will keep out of it, but Justine will be pleased, and from what I can see, Christmas is all about her this year.

When he reveals his plans, I'm startled.

'Round John virgin, mother and Kyle,' I sing, and Justine grins. It's one of our favourite games to see how many wrong words we can sneak into carols. A tradition that deserved to die years back. My sister wins when 'the cattle are blowing the poor baby away' evades detection.

'I think we should do "Ding Dong Merrily on High",' Mum says. 'We can sing it in a round.'

Dad looks bored. He'd be happier with a glass of wine. Gran is in the other room with the telly on full blast, shouting abuse at celebrity antique hunters.

'Don't buy that table, you lanky gobshites. Buy the fecking vase.'

The doorbell goes, and Mum looks annoyed. 'Who can that be?'

'Neighbours begging us to stop singing?' Justine says.

'The nearest house is a mile away.'

Mum goes to see, and I hold my breath.

Footsteps retreat down the hall. The front door opens, voices mumble, and then raise.

'Look who it is,' Mum says in her trying-not-to-freak-out voice.

'John,' I cry and gather my brother in a warm embrace. Justine does the same. Mum and Dad gather awkwardly, watching like outsiders.

Gran pokes her head around the door. 'I thought I heard voices.'

John hands me a cigarette. I should let him know I gave

up six months back, but I take it anyway. Mum pretends not to watch from the kitchen window. She blames me for this. I half expected him to bring Katherine, but she's visiting her family.

On Christmas morning, we gather around the tree. Somehow, John's unexpected arrival has been forgotten. Forgiven, even. But now comes the awkward bit. The exchange of gifts, and he'll be left empty-handed.

'This is for you,' Mum says and hands me an envelope.

'Money,' I say and kiss her cheek. 'How lovely. It's just what I always wanted.'

Justine gets a scarf. Money's too high-risk. She could easily trade it for booze.

Gran hands out bobble hats. John gets one, and he's so overcome that he puts it on and dances around the tree.

'It's nice to see someone appreciate all my hard work,' Gran says. 'I've arthritis in my fingers.'

Guilt-tripped, we all don lopsided hats.

'Right then,' Dad says. 'I suppose I'm on potato-peeling duty.'

He heads for the kitchen before anyone can suggest he hang out and enjoy more family time.

It's Mum's first real chance to attack.

'What are you doing here?' she hisses at my brother. 'You know how much it hurts your father.'

He looks at me for support, and I pray he'll not land me in it.

'Gran invited me.'

All eyes turn on her.

'That's right,' she says. 'And why shouldn't I ask my grandson?'

Mum's face burns red with rage. 'Because you don't have a grandson.'

'So, who's this lad in front of me?'

'Fine,' she says. 'Let's all pretend and play happy families.'

She doesn't allow us the long-brewing showdown, instead heading into the kitchen.

'I shouldn't have come.' John sounds mournful.

'You've as much right as anyone to be here,' I say, and Justine rests her head on his shoulder.

'Don't let them chase you away. I've been there. It's no fun.'

Gran passes me her teacup, and I fill it with vodka. Big measures, we agreed. Essential after the day just gone. John is asleep next door with Justine. I put my head around the door and saw them curled around each other. Like when they were tiny. Except, obviously, not quite. Mum and Dad are still downstairs watching *The Great Escape* with the sound up full. If they turned it down, there might be room to talk, which would never do.

The following day, there's a strange atmosphere. Like everyone has a hangover.

'I suppose my brother is out jogging or something,' Justine says as I hand her a morning cup of tea.

An alarm bell rings in my head.

'I thought he was still in your bed.'

'He got up around eight-thirty.'

I go into the hall and see the empty coat peg. He's gone.

Gran is next down, and I try to keep the truth to myself.

'It's a lovely day,' she says. 'Fine and dry.'

Justine pours tea. 'John has gone out for a run. He puts the rest of us to shame.'

Gran glances at me and then away again. 'I suppose my daughter is having a lie-in. God knows what time they went to bed.'

'I heard the telly go off at three,' Justine says. 'I dare say Dad passed out long before.'

Gran forces a smile, walks over to the window and stares into patchwork fields that fall away from the end of her garden. How I loved growing up here. As children, the three of us would run through the woods, playing hide and seek. We turned the barn into a theatre and put on shows for anyone who cared to be our audience.

Gran reaches into her pocket.

'This is for you,' she says, handing Justine an envelope. 'There's one for Laura too.'

We both know what it will be.

I open mine first, read the first line, and tears cloud my eyes.

I stay in the garden and try lip-reading through the kitchen window. Mum's face says one thing, but her body language suggests something else. It's just like her, she'll be saying. Trying to make everything about her.

And why not? I wonder.

All any of us want is love.

I hadn't planned to work the few days between Christmas and New Year. Officially, the office is closed, but my pass allows 24-hour access, and I need to be away from an empty flat.

Marie from Accounts sits at her desk.

'I was sick of the in-laws,' she says. 'Nothing's ever good enough.'

We go for lunch together. It's fine and dry, and we sit on a bench and eat Pret A Manger Christmas dinner sandwiches.

'I have a fridge full of turkey,' Marie says. 'Why am I buying more?'

All I've done since getting in a taxi for the station is

dwell on how Mum screamed after me as I told her what I thought, how she had no right to deny John his life. Just because he wasn't who she wanted him to be.

'How was your Christmas?' I ask Marie. 'I mean, really.'

She shrugs.

'Quiet is what I think they expect you to say. What about you?'

'Too quiet. Everybody tiptoeing around each other in case feelings got hurt.'

Marie knows about John. I told her two years ago when we sat and drank brandy at the office party.

'Did your brother come?'

'Gran invited him.'

'Jesus, how did that go down?'

'Like a cup of cold sick.'

'He's still her kid,' she says. 'I think that's how I'd feel about it.'

John calls on New Year's Eve and tells me about how Katherine has suggested they move to Amsterdam. It's a tolerant place, apparently. If you grew up one sex and became another, nobody bats an eyelid.

'I'll be good dinner-party conversation,' he laughs.

I laugh, too, but feel so utterly sad. Almost dead inside. 'Will you tell Mum and Dad?'

There's a long silence before he speaks. 'I always want them to be in my life.'

'They'll never visit.'

'But you will?'

'Of course.'

'You remember that year when you bought me a cardigan?'

I rack my brain. 'The green one?'

'That's the yoke. I still have it. It still fits me.'

'Mum hit the roof,' I say.

'I suppose that was when I realised she'd never really accept what I needed to do with my life. And I knew you already did.'

'She'll maybe come around...'

John cuts me off. 'She probably won't, but that's OK now. I had an email this morning... from Dad.'

I'm more shocked that Dad even knows how to send emails than the fact he got in touch.

'What did he say?'

'Goodbye, Louise. I hope you'll stay happy.' He addressed the envelope to John Evans.

A lump catches in my throat. 'Next year, we'll do Christmas in Amsterdam.'

'Bring Gran and Justine.'

'We won't be allowed a drink.'

'Like this year?' he laughs. 'I guessed what you two were up to in that bedroom.'

After putting down the phone, I turn the sound back up on the TV: Jools Holland and a bunch of people seeing in the new year. Gran is asleep in her chair, and Justine's raiding the fridge for leftovers.

'We should go for a walk tomorrow,' she calls through. 'Did they say what the weather will be?'

'Fine and dry,' I say and smile to myself. 'Fine and dry.'

Reunion

You'd be late for your own funeral. That's what Emily's mother used to say. And she was right. But Emily has a plan. Years of burned dinners, missed appointments, and parking tickets end here. This Christmas.

She's made a list. She's checked it twice.

Everything is ready for the best family Christmas ever.

It's taken three shopping trips to get everything. And that was a trial. Emily hates shopping. Or rather, she hates shoppers. People push in, or stand behind you and mutter about how slow the girl behind the counter is going. This season of goodwill isn't universal.

She surveys the spread.

Everyone will be here at seven, they said. That's more than enough time to get the house shipshape.

This year, she won't scrabble in the loft for the tree while a still-frozen turkey floats in a warm bath. She got the tree down yesterday and stuck it together with plumbing tape. There's enough tinsel, ribbons and baubles to hide her repairs.

'Everyone's dressing their trees in white,' Sophie told her last year. 'You really ought to consider getting an actual tree.'

'They make too much mess,' Emily said. 'And this one has been in the family since you were born.'

Her daughter exchanged looks with her husband: chinless James—the bored bank manager who slept with his secretary two years back. But we found it in our hearts to forgive. Or rather, Sophie did. Emily still can't look him in the eye.

The presents are wrapped in silver and gold. She got the paper from a lovely little shop in a quiet lane. The man behind the counter seemed thrilled to sell it. And it made her think twice about the state of this world.

Sophie and James have promised to call on their way to the airport. The lucky devils. Two weeks in the sun. Away from the cold. The slush. The rain. The wind whistles around loose-fitting panes.

'I don't know if I could enjoy a turkey dinner when it's hot outside,' Emily said when they eventually told her their plan.

Sophie laughed. 'We'll probably have sushi by the pool.'

'What about the kids? Won't they miss Santa?'

'Lauren and Harry are staying with Barbara.'

'That'll be nice. They ought to spend more time with their other grandma.'

'We've had to promise to bring her a crate of local wine back,' chinless James said.

The best Stourbridge crystal looks lovely. Today feels like a day for these glasses. And champagne. The good stuff is usually hidden behind John's lawnmower in the garage, waiting for a special occasion.

And this will be that.

The plastic centrepiece summons thoughts of a wintry afternoon when Sophie and Ben were six. They'd taken the dogs for a walk. It was freezing, and Ben chucked sticks as Holly gathered mistletoe.

Back home, the kids ran to find John.

'Look what we found, Dad,' Sophie said. 'Kiss me now.'

John put down his newspaper and laughed.

How Emily missed that.

It's time to get changed. The white dress has hung on the back of the bedroom door since Tuesday. The day she braved trying it on. How pleased she was to find that weeks of denial meant it fitted after all these years.

Emily's made a list. Now she's checking it twice.

She won't need shoes.

Or lipstick.

Or the wig.

She recalls how John would fasten her necklace and let his lips linger. How he'd whisper something filthy and suggest they stay home.

'Let's make an excuse.'

'I promised Sophie.'

'She'll be too busy with her fancy friends. I really can't face a room of assistant bank managers.'

'They'll have gone to a lot of trouble.'

'It'll be things on sticks. That won't fill me up. We must stop for chips on the way home.'

Emily turned her head to taste his mouth. Stale wine edged with a hint of brandy. And cigarettes.

'Have you been smoking?'

'I only had one.'

'You promised.'

The phone rings. She lets the machine pick up. Why

have a dog and bark yourself? It's Sophie. As expected, with this year's excuse.

'Mum, are you there? Pick up. We'll be with you in about half an hour.'

There is a brief pause; then the line goes dead.

That's a turn-up for the books. She's coming. It makes everything so much better. Reunions can be tricky when half the people don't show.

The doorbell will play 'White Christmas'.

The man in the pound shop laughed when she bought it.

'That'll drive you mad by Boxing Day,' he said.

She didn't tell him she was halfway there.

The cork leaves the bottle with a satisfying pop. John taught her how to open champagne: turn the bottle, not the cork. She last drank it on the day they promised she was in remission.

They'd taken away the lump and expected her to be happy.

It didn't matter that they'd taken away her hair and smile.

'To the future,' John said.

And if she'd had any idea how short that future would be, she'd have drunk it slowly.

When the car left the road, time grew sticky.

Lights drifted past the windows.

John's hand found hers as his face fell to pieces.

Ben lay out of reach on the back seat.

Sobbing.

Calling for her.

Then wheezing.

Then nothing.

She opens the kitchen drawer and pulls out three silver-wrapped boxes.

One for Sophie. One for Ben. And one for John.

It's time.

One by one.

Each white tablet is washed away with fine champagne.

Sophie and chinless James will be here soon.

The phone rings again.

Surely not.

She wishes she'd got one of those machines that showed the number.

The outgoing message plays, and then Sophie speaks.

'We wanted to see you before we went,' she says. 'But it's been on the radio, the M25 is rammed, and if we leave it any later, we could miss our flight, and then you'd be stuck with us for Christmas.'

Emily smiles first at John and then at Ben.

Some things never change.

Some things you can count on.

It won't be long now.

How Long Has It Been?

This is adapted from drafts for what was then my upcoming novel 'Rebuilding Alexandra Small' and gives you an insight into the back story creation involved in writing a new book. None of this has made the final draft, but I wanted to share it here given the seasonal setting.

A year and a half ago, I ran out of reasons not to join my husband for his office Christmas party. We were booked into a suite in a fancy hotel, with a minibar.

'I've been sober for two years,' I said with a sigh.

Jed looked ashamed. 'I forgot to tell them at reception.'

I sat on the edge of the bed. 'It's fine. I'll be happy with the Toblerone.'

He picked up the phone on the nightstand and called down. Minutes later, someone appeared with a trolley and stripped the tiny fridge of temptation.

'Do you have plans for the afternoon?' Jed said when we were alone again.

I looked up from my laptop. 'First up, finish this report.'

'You're officially on holiday.'

'Yeah, but if I don't send this out today, Sam will be on the warpath.'

'Right,' he said. 'How about I keep you company? I'll feed you Toblerone and make tea.'

'Whatever,' I said, going back to my work. 'But we can't dick about. I need to concentrate.'

For a while, he lounged on a long leather banquette and pretended to read the book that had been on the floor under his side of the bed for almost a year. Whenever I looked up, he was staring.

'More tea, vicar?' he said.

'Why don't you see if anyone wants to play snooker? I'm almost done. We could go for a swim later. The pool looks great.'

It worked. He left me in peace.

I was trying to import a chart into my presentation when he returned.

'So much for the swimming pool.' He sounded cross. 'Shall I run you a bath?'

I glanced at the clock on my computer. Somehow, I'd lost track of four hours.

'Sorry, I lost myself,' I said.

'We need to be downstairs for the drinks reception in an hour.'

My stomach growled. I'd eaten four triangles of mountain-shaped chocolate since breakfast. The Tesco Local opposite called my name.

'Will there be food at this reception?' I said. 'Or is it an excuse for a piss-up?'

Jed sat on the bed and lifted away my laptop. 'We'll order room service later.'

I jumped into the shower and changed into a black silk slip dress.

'You look fabulous.' He kissed my neck and fastened the clasp on a red wooden necklace.

'Promise I can bail early if everybody gets slaughtered,' I said.

He laughed and kissed me again. 'We've got a sales meeting at 9.30, so it won't be a late one.'

I smiled. 'Famous last words.'

As we walked into the ballroom, Jed swooped on the only tray of orange juice.

'I'll stay sober too,' he said. 'Solidarity and all that.'

I shook my head. 'You're OK to have a few drinks.'

He handed me both glasses. 'Great. This should keep you going for a while.'

'For a while?'

'My boss needs us for a strategy meeting.'

'You're leaving me on my own?' I scanned the noisy room. 'Why didn't you say? I'd have stayed upstairs and watched *Coronation Street*.'

Jed backed away, his smile wide. 'I promise we won't be long.'

I headed for the bar, the best place to hide. Everyone was too obsessed about missing their turn to notice me.

Someone tapped my arm. 'Evie, what a lovely surprise.'

Lou Taylor, queen of the work wives, looked like she'd rolled in body glitter and frilled cotton. She leaned in for air kisses.

'Come and meet the others,' she said, and much as I'd have rather faked my death, I followed.

The wives acted super-cheery, shuffling their bony bums along a velvet sofa to make room for my ample arse.

Lou proposed a toast.

'To a great sales conference,' she said, then clasped a hand over her mouth as her eyes widened. 'Sophie, you must think I'm awful, making a toast like that. You can't even join in because you're an alkie. I forgot.'

Everyone stared at me.

'How do you do the whole sober thing?' one of them said — the question they always ask. 'I'd go loopy without a drink.'

'It's this or die,' I said.

A line of sympathetic heads cocked.

'Talk about putting a downer on Christmas,' Lou groaned. 'God, Sophie, cheer up.'

'I'm fine,' I said through gritted teeth.

'Just because you're an alkie, it's no excuse to spoil the fun for the rest of us.'

'Can you say "alkie"?' someone whispered. 'Isn't that like calling a Black boy "coloured"?'

'I still enjoy myself,' I said. 'I don't need to drink, that's all.'

They put down their glasses one by one, determined to show solidarity with their sober sister. But not Lou. Her plumped lips formed a grim line, and she leaned back, smirking.

'I don't need to drink, that's all,' she repeated, trying to sound like me.

I reached for my glass. 'I might go for a wander.'

'Because you're better than us?' she said.

I took a swig of bitter orange juice. My mouth watered. 'If I've hurt or upset any of you, please accept my apology and enjoy your evening.'

I was hiding near the bar when Jed reappeared from a side room.

'You smell of smoke,' I said.

'They handed out Cuban cigars.' He pulled one from his pocket. 'Your glass is empty.'

He merged with a queuing crowd, leaving me exposed.

'Nobody likes her,' a little voice said. One of the other wives. 'Lou assumes we're the best of mates, but that's not true.'

I nodded, but the words got stuck.

Jed returned with a flute of fizzy water. 'Introduce me.'

'I'm Faith. Harry's wife.'

'Faith never normally comes to these things either,' Jed said. 'You've got loads in common.'

She blushed and stared at the floor as Jed waved at someone and ducked away again.

Faith spoke in a voice so small I struggled to hear.

'How long has it been for you?' she said when I leaned in. 'I'm three months on Friday.'

I jerked back, surprised. 'What about that glass of champagne?'

'I didn't touch it.'

A squeal of static turned all heads to the stage as Lou tapped the microphone.

'Can everybody hear me?' she said. 'Let's turn up the lights.' Her eyes searched the crowd. 'Tonight's a special night. We're blessed by a royal visit.'

Faint gasps. Rumours rippled — Elton John again. Last year we got someone who used to read traffic reports on local radio.

'Show us your tits!' a male voice jeered.

Others wolf-whistled. I slipped deeper into shadow.

'Where is she?' Lou demanded. 'Where's Sophie?'

Hands pulled me out of hiding.

'Come on down,' she trilled, as polite applause forced me along the aisle.

When the clapping died, she took a deep breath.

'Ladies and gentlemen, at Christmas we often forget how much sadness exists in the world.'

In my head, I made a hundred deals with God: fire alarm, sprinklers, faulty electrics — anything.

'How long has it been, Sophie?' she said, pushing the mic into my face.

I didn't answer fast enough.

'How long since the stomach pump?'

I mumbled something about two years and snatched the mic.

'I used to love parties,' I said. 'Drinking myself silly. Nine times out of ten, I woke up wondering what died in my mouth.'

A few people laughed.

'But tonight, someone told me I act like I'm better than the rest of you because I've been sober two years — and that's not true.' I swallowed a hard lump of tears. 'I stayed away because I don't consider myself good enough.'

The lights dimmed. No need to see their shamed faces.

Lou lunged for the mic, but I dodged.

'I'm only here tonight because of one man.'

The room relaxed. Sophie Fox — the drunk who made good — about to thank her adoring husband.

Jed pushed through the crowd. Our eyes locked.

'We're trying for a baby,' I said.

And the room exploded.

French Leave

How different things are this Christmas. So English, after six years cut off from the homeland. Last year, I cooked a chicken bought with spare change from our neighbours. Monsieur Hedin had his mother pluck the bird while I drank coffee and watched her crouch on the stone steps, ripping feathers from its lifeless body.

'Would you like it prepared for roasting?' he asked.

I nodded, and she produced a knife, hacked off its head and feet, then reached inside to yank out the bloody entrails.

I boiled it in a dented copper pot, fingers crossed, willing the gas to last the day. Jean-Michel, who delivered bottles, was away visiting friends. The last thing I needed was a half-cooked Frankenstein chicken.

I imagined that would be my forever life, until Ben's father died and we came back to the UK for a visit that turned into a temporary stay... and then became permanent.

Our family swapped Le Pays des Sept Vallées for Kent

— the Garden of England. The country lanes look the same, except now I have to remember to drive on the other side of the road.

On the upside, I get to buy chickens ready-plucked.

Ben's boss was brilliant. The company kept him on.

Matthew started at the local school. It's lovely, but the headmistress explained she likes all the mums and dads to get involved. Being a suck-up, I nodded with sage enthusiasm and found myself volunteering to oversee the nativity.

'What were you thinking?' Ben said on the drive home.

'I need new friends. It might help.'

'Does this mean I have to come and watch it?'

'I've got you down to help with wardrobe.'

He shook his head, smiling. 'I'll do what I can.'

Neither of us reckoned with Fiona Denby-Smythe — self-appointed leader of the mums. Super-Mum. She took umbrage after hearing me babble in French on the phone to Madame Hedin.

'I didn't know you spoke French, Laura.'

'We lived there for a while.'

The smile reached her lips but not her eyes. 'I'm more of a Spanish speaker. We have a timeshare in Andalusia.'

She pronounced it with a lisp.

I held up my clipboard. 'Can I count you in for the nativity?'

'Count me in?'

'I'm looking for volunteers.'

Fiona looked around for support. 'Are you under the impression you're in charge?'

'I was asked—'

She cut me short. 'All events go through the social committee, and as head of said committee, I don't recall any discussion.'

The headmistress must have seen what was going on, because she intervened.

'I've asked Laura to step in this year — share the load, so to speak. You're always so busy with the Christmas fair and carol service.'

Fiona's lips formed a hard line. 'Many hands make light work.'

'Exactly. And I'm sure Laura will welcome any tips you can hand down.'

'Absolutely,' I said, trying for the right level of deference.

'Fresh blood.' Fiona waved dismissively. 'Best she makes her own mistakes.'

The day tickets went on sale, two mums set up a table near the cloakroom.

'Here she is,' one clucked as I tried to sneak past unseen. 'The producer.'

'How are sales going?' I asked brightly.

'Slow. It's always such a nightmare finding babysitters. All the good ones are snapped up. Stragglers make do with some feral waif from the council estate who hasn't a hope of passing her DBS check.'

'Well, I suppose I'd best get one for my better half.'

They exchanged glances. 'Won't he be backstage?'

'Ben spends half the week in France.'

They stared like I'd said something odd.

'So... shall I get a ticket?' I rummaged for money.

'Front row,' the mum in charge said. 'He'll see everything.'

Ten quid feels steep for a nativity that'll last half an

hour, but I'm assured it includes a mince pie and something gorgeous to drink. I paid up.

Matthew got a non-speaking role — desperate to avoid accusations of favouritism.

On the afternoon of the show, Fiona cornered me and enveloped me in air-kiss theatre.

'It's rare to see you at this sort of thing.'

'What sort of thing?'

'You're most welcome. But I couldn't help noticing you've placed your better half on the front row.'

'Producer's perk,' I said, smiling tight.

'Remind me — what role did Matthew get?'

'He's a sheep.'

She clicked her tongue. 'Julia's daughter is a shepherd. She has a line. Best they swap seats.'

I spotted Julia looking mortified. I caved.

Ben found his assigned seat in the darkest corner of the hall — next to the caretaker's mops.

'It smells of sick,' he whispered. 'And there's a draught.'

'Just remember to take a photo.'

Half an hour later, Ben was on his feet, cheering for more.

Other parents stared, but sod them. One proud father — that's what matters.

'Can we go for pizza?' Matthew asked as we left.

'I thought you wanted Nando's?'

'Yeah, but we could go to Pizza Express.'

Ben ignored my warning eyes. 'Pizza it is.'

I poked him in the ribs. 'Pizza Express is the official after-party. Competitive Chardonnay drinking. Awards. Tears.'

'Awards?'

'What for — best barnyard animal?'

Fiona pounced the moment we slipped inside.

'I didn't think this was your scene, Laura.'

'Matthew wanted to come.'

'How darling. Such a good little boy, supporting his friends with proper roles.'

'Yeah,' I said. 'But it's not like it was a competition. It was a nativity play. The girl who played Mary wet herself.'

Fiona's smile froze. She flapped away.

Matthew didn't win best barnyard animal. Fiona's awards were full-Oscar — complete with lengthy acceptance speeches from parents thanking the British Museum.

'How did that strangely tall lad win best zebra?' I said as Ben buckled Matthew into the car. 'Did they even have zebras in Bethlehem?'

Matthew showed me his 'Good Sport' certificate.

'I won too,' he beamed. I kissed his forehead.

Ben stiffened. 'Fiona alert.'

Too late. Fiona grabbed my elbow.

'Super to catch you before you slipped away. About parking...'

My stomach knotted.

'I noticed your Volvo in the disabled space on Thursday.'

'Ben had a flight. I was there for two minutes.'

'What if someone in a wheelchair needed it? It's not a great message, is it?'

I forced a nod. 'You're right. I'm sorry.'

'Minor point, best made. We'll see you at the Christmas fair? I noticed you haven't signed up — perhaps you'd like second-hand sports kit?'

She swivelled and tottered away.

'I hate them all,' I muttered as Ben started the car. 'A bunch of bitches. And she's the worst.'

'Bunch of bitches,' Matthew echoed sleepily.

'I meant they're strictly grown-up words, darling.'

'But Daddy said that lady is a shit-stirrer.'

I sighed into my glass later. Ben poured more wine.

'We could change schools,' he said. 'St Chad's?'

'Knife crime is down,' I deadpanned.

'Perhaps not then.'

'Fiona has volunteered me onto the Valentine's Ball committee.'

'A ball? For five-year-olds?'

'I have to book a band and find a cupid.'

'How about your father? Is he still taking off his clothes in Tesco?'

'The doctor upped his tablets. But Mum said he unbuttoned in the freezer aisle last Tuesday.'

Ben retrieved an envelope from beneath the tree.

'You deserve this now.'

'Won't it spoil the surprise?'

'Open it.'

He must have seen me glance guiltily towards the other gifts.

'You'll still get the oven gloves from Matthew,' he said. 'And the robot vacuum you dropped hints about.'

I unwrapped the paper. It was from his French employer.

'They've made you redundant?' Panic rose. 'What now?'

'Read it again — the bit at the end.'

All I saw was a number.

A huge number.

'Do we have to pay it back?'

'It's my pay-off.'

'They're giving us all that?'

'If we move back to France. They want me as a consultant — part-time, but enough. They asked for volunteers.'

My heart skipped. For months we'd insisted Kent was perfect — that we were putting down roots.

'So we step back in time?' I said.

'It's too good to miss.'

'But why?'

'When did you last smile?'

I curled into him. 'What do we do when the money runs out?'

'Same as always. We manage.'

Outside, the first flakes drifted. The heating clunked and hummed. I could stand up now, boil the kettle — knowing it will work, knowing the water will run.

In whatever tumbledown French villa we land in next, there may be none of that.

And I've never felt more alive.

The best gift ever.

The Gift Exchange

I've sometimes been asked what became of Lisa Doyle, the main character from my first novel, *The Armchair Bride*. So here's a short story for Christmas to update you on her life these days. Two years on from the end of that book, Lisa's home with Brian for a family Christmas and about to encounter a ghost from the past!

Mam looks up from the Christmas cards gathered on the kitchen table.

"Do you have an address for Ginny?" she asks. "Last thing I heard, she moved into one of those new flats near the precinct."

"You're not seriously sending her a card?" I try to keep my voice even. "After everything she did."

"It's a time to forgive."

"She almost got me killed."

Mam shakes her head. "It was a toy gun."

"Nobody knew that."

"Guru Westwood says you have to forgive to move on."

Mam scribbles a greeting on the card. "Life's too short to hold grudges."

Two months ago, Mam saw a flyer in the library for The Golden Buddha Trust—a group for retired people in search of "answers to life's many questions." These days, she loves everyone—except for Muriel across the street, who never puts the lid on her recycling bin.

The front door closes, and Brian dumps the oversized bag I insisted he pack in the hall.

"Do you need anything else from the car?" he asks. "I've left Amy and Sue's presents in the boot like you said."

Mam rolls her eyes. "What's wrong with putting gifts under the tree?"

"They'll keep prodding at them. Let's have surprises this year."

Both Mam and Brian stare at my belly—my huge, eight-month pregnant belly.

"I think I've already had my share of surprises," she says. "Haven't there been enough secrets in this family?"

I found out I was expecting Lucinda on my forty-second birthday. Brian held my hand as a nurse smeared gel over my distended stomach, and we stared at the monitor to make sense of random light patterns.

"Do you want to know the sex?" the nurse asked, and before Brian could answer, I said yes. I've never been good with surprises.

The name came two days later.

"I read somewhere that the first name you think of is the right one and that you should write it down," I told him, producing a scrap of paper from my pocket. On it, I'd written "Lucinda."

Brian peered at it. "When did you do that?"

I had planned to act mysteriously and insist the name

materialized in a dream, spoken by angelic voices. Lucinda was my Nan's name, and Dad once made me promise to consider it if grandchildren ever came my way.

"It's been in my head a while," I said.

"Lucinda?" Brian made the name sound like one he'd never heard. "It's cute. Lucy for short."

I enjoyed the smug feeling of someone who knew best. Lucinda was a noble name, one not open for teasing.

The doorbell rings, and Brian is sent to answer. I hear voices and then a scratching at the door. Bertie pushes his nose around and dives into the bags gathered around my feet.

"Does this dog ever stop?" I cry as Mam laughs.

"Give him a biscuit," she says. "He loves digestives."

The mere mention of the word "biscuit" has Bertie on his haunches, brown eyes burning into mine.

My sister drags two reluctant offspring into the kitchen.

"Isn't Amy here yet?" she asks, and everyone exchanges awkward looks.

"Glen has business to tend to," Mam mutters darkly. "Special business."

Sue gets it at once, and even though her face flushes, she manages to smile.

Most families would applaud charity work. That one of their kin wants to give up time to hand out gifts to orphans and the homeless should be a good thing. And maybe Mam would be on board with this had Glen agreed to disguise himself as Santa Claus or even as an elf—his insistence on dressing up as Susan Boyle has her on edge.

"What time is that nonsense over?" Mam asks.

"Amy reckoned they'll be here by five," I say, looking anxiously around. All I want to do is change the subject before she launches into another distinctly unforgiving, un-Buddhist rant.

I'm too late.

"Don't get me wrong. I've tried to understand," she says. "But it has me stumped. I sometimes wonder if I'd have been happier if he had been having an affair. Having a father who gets his jollies by wearing women's knickers... Well, it's not the right environment for a child."

"How can you say that?" Sue jumps in to defend Glen and Amy. "Tishiba is the luckiest little girl living."

"There's that name again," Mam says. "She sounds like they should stand her in the electrics department of John Lewis."

The door goes again, and Bertie runs barking into the hall.

Brian goes to answer.

"Probably carol singers," Mam says. "I had a group round last night. They couldn't hold a tune in a bucket."

When he comes back, Brian looks worried.

"It's for you," he says. "It's Ginny."

When I last saw Ginny Baker, she wore a tight red dress and expensive heels. She'd been picking her way through the debris of an almost-ruined wedding, and I told myself that would be the last time we spoke. But even then, a tiny voice inside warned that things remained unfinished.

The woman perched on Mam's sofa in the Good Room is almost unrecognizable. The long blonde hair has been cut short and left to grow out dark. The expensive makeup is a thing of the past.

This Ginny regards me with empty eyes.

"I'm dying," she says with no preamble. "Someone told me you were down for Christmas, so I thought I'd come along and tell you firsthand. Save you hearing it from someone else."

"My God," I say. "Are you all right?"

"Didn't you hear what I said? I'm dying."

"What of?"

"Cancer. Is there anything else these days?"

She shifts uneasily, and pain flickers across her face.

"Breast, metastatic into my bones. It's incurable. They've said weeks, not months."

"I'm so sorry."

She nods. "People usually are."

An awkward silence is broken when Mam pops her head around the door to offer cups of tea. Ginny pulls a bottle from her bag and swallows a cocktail of tablets.

"Those tablets," I say. "They must think there's hope."

She winces. "It manages the pain and ticks a box somewhere."

I want to argue. Has she exhausted every sort of treatment? Can I help?

"I caused trouble for you, didn't I?" Ginny says.

I make myself smile, patting my tummy. "It's all sorted out now. We're fine. Everything's fine."

"And you even tried to make friends with me," she says. "That day when..."

"Yes, well, never mind. It was a strange old day, I suppose. We all said things we regret."

"Actually, Lisa, I didn't." Ginny gets up and walks to the window. "I'm glad I didn't give you what you wanted."

"OK," I say, unsure where this might be going.

"I needed to get away from here. It was what I always dreamed of doing, and... you allowed me to escape. Right after that wedding, I got into my car and drove. All the way to London."

"Someone told me that's where you were living."

"I had a good few years, all things considered." Ginny stops talking, turns around, and looks at me. "I've come here to thank you."

"Thank me?"

"I was the one holding me back. I blamed everyone else, but it was me all along. You made me see that."

Ginny sips from a tiny glass of red wine and watches everyone open gifts, try on slippers and gloves, spray each other with perfume, and hand around expensive chocolates.

"You did a nice thing," Brian says as he puts an arm around me. "Inviting her to stay for dinner."

I nod slowly. "She's not quite the monster I thought."

Bertie barks, and the kids play tag. Mam sits in her chair, enjoying the love of her family, and even Glen is permitted a smile despite the fluffy pink mules he insists on wearing—a gift from Amy.

The ambulance arrives at six thirty, just after Mam loads the dishwasher.

"You're calling her Lucinda?" Ginny says as I help her into a wheelchair. "Loo rhymes with poo. That poor kid. Bullies will make her life hell. If I give you nothing else, take it from someone who knows."

She laughs a raspy, wheezy rattle.

As they pull away, Brian slips an arm around me.

"OK?" he asks, and I nod. There's the smallest of kicks inside, and I know what I have to do.

"Sophie's a lovely name, isn't it?" I say. "Maybe we should rethink the whole Lucinda thing."

Ernie's First Christmas

Being a dog is cool. You get to lick the kitchen floor and nobody really minds.

They think it's cute.

The big people came back from shopping with strange smiles on their faces. The one who usually wears the pretty dress said something about how I had to be good, and if I was the best boy ever, then there might be a big surprise. My first thought was steak, or a bone, or even some of those yummy sausages they get from the fancy shop in the village — the one I have to sit outside of while they buy stuff.

Pretty Dress laughed, so I did my doggy duty and rolled on my back to let her tickle my tum.

But then the one with short hair called from outside. He sounded out of breath and ever so slightly annoyed.

Pretty Dress stopped what she was doing.

'What's Daddy up to?' she laughed, running to the window. 'Gosh, Ernie, look at silly Daddy. He'll never get that through the front door.'

From the hall came grunts and groans. Short Hair called for help.

I followed Pretty Dress outside.

Short Hair was standing in the garden with what looked like a tree. He looked so proud of himself.

I crept over, head down low, and sniffed.

You know how they teach you at puppy school that if something looks like a duck and quacks, it most likely *is* a duck? Same thing with trees. And that was what he had dragged home.

A tree.

Not a pretty tree with floaty leaves and sticky branches. This was a funny-looking thing with spikes and a funky smell.

'Give me a hand getting it inside,' Short Hair said.

I barked because it seemed like such a funny thing to suggest.

But they were serious, and between them they dragged it through the hall and into the good room.

They seemed so proud as they sat on the sofa looking at it, so I made a doggy executive decision to let this bit of strangeness go.

I wasn't like Scruff, who lived two doors down. He used to overthink everything. He insisted that Pretty Dress was a silly name for any human.

'What happens when she wears trousers?' he once said.

'What matters is what she had on when we first met,' I explained. 'And that was a very pretty dress. Blue and green with swirly shapes.'

Scruff didn't get it at all. But he was six years old, which is ancient in dog years.

Pretty Dress jumped to her feet.

'I should put away the shopping,' she said, so I went with her to snuffle through the bags and see what else was on offer.

I must have fallen asleep in my basket because the next thing I knew, they were calling my name.

'Ernie!' It was Short Hair. 'Ernie, come see this.'

It was dark outside, so I assumed it must be dinner, and I got up, stretched, and made my doggy way down the hall.

Pretty Dress stood by the door.

'Hey there, boy,' she said. I wish she wouldn't call me that. 'Come see your first Christmas tree.'

In the corner of the room, right where I liked my basket to be, was the funky-smelling tree. Except now it looked... fancy. Covered with sparkles and shiny balls.

'What do you think?' Short Hair said. 'Isn't it cool?'

What did I think?

They'd dragged home a tree and covered it in... stuff.

I thought they needed their heads examined.

They looked so happy that I barked and wagged my tail.

'Ernie loves it,' Short Hair said.

He was always the slower one of the two.

They watched the telly box that evening, and because their funny tree took up my corner, I had to sleep on the rug. Have you ever tried sleeping through shouting and firing guns?

I wasn't happy.

So I decided. It was me or the tree.

'You'll be a good boy, won't you?' Pretty Dress said. 'Daddy and me are going for drinks with friends. Can we trust you on your own?'

Short Hair muttered something I won't repeat. Not suitable for young ears. I curled up and shut my eyes like I was tired and ready to sleep.

I waited until I was sure they were gone — then jumped up.

First, I needed help, so I padded to the kitchen and called for Mortimer.

He poked his mousey nose from behind the bin.

'What gives, dude?' he said.

'They've brought a tree home.'

He looked at me like I'd made it up.

'A tree?'

'Yes, and they've put it in *my* corner.'

He scurried to check.

'Dude, they put a tree in your corner,' he confirmed. 'What do we do?'

He rested his mousy head on his mousy paw and thought.

'How would you feel about me subcontracting things?'

I eyed him with suspicion.

'As long as it's not to a cat.'

He rolled his eyes.

'Do I strike you as a guy who hangs out with cats?'

We high-fived, and away he scuttled.

I went back to the good room and studied the tree. I suppose it was pretty, but a dog's corner is a dog's corner.

A few minutes later, I heard voices. Mortimer was back with a buck-toothed fluffy guy with a long ginger tail.

'This is Squiggly,' he said. 'He knows a thing or two about trees.'

Squiggly followed us in and whipped out a tape measure.

'This is a major job,' he said. 'Three squirrels at least. Even then, we can't make any promises. Did you consider beavers?'

Mortimer pulled a face.

'And where would I find a beaver in Brighton?'

Squiggly scratched his chin.

'Do you have a saw?'

'A sore what?' I said. They both laughed.

'The guy's just a pup,' Mortimer said.

I pretended to laugh too.

After more measuring, they left.

I paced the room.

Pretty Dress and Short Hair could be back any minute. I had to take matters into my own paws.

I gnawed carefully at one of the shiny balls. It came away and bounced across the floor. This would be easy.

I pulled them off one by one until I couldn't reach any more. I cleared a branch big enough to get a grip and pull.

At first, the tree rattled. More stuff tumbled. Then, as my paws slipped across the wooden floor, it moved. Slowly at first... then very quickly.

'Dude, you should have waited,' Squiggly said. 'Me and the boys would have taken care of things.'

He was with six other squirrels, all in baseball caps, all looking miffed.

'I promised these guys payment,' he said, nodding to the bowl of satsumas and walnuts by the fireplace.

What choice did I have?

They took all they could carry and scuttled away.

Mortimer shook his head.

'How do we play this, Ernie? Either way, you could be sent to the dog's home.'

I'd heard about the dog's home. Cold floors. No heating. Rocks and twigs for dinner. And every few days, they take dogs away and they never come back.

I didn't have time to think. Pretty Dress and Short Hair were back. I heard their voices in the hall.

Mortimer vanished in a flash.

I was alone.

They came into the room, bright-eyed and laughing — but then they stopped dead.

Short Hair looked annoyed and said rude words.

Pretty Dress laughed.

They looked around… then at me. I did my best cheesy grin and wagged my tail more than any pup ever wagged.

The silence hurt.

I saw my future — a concrete floor and a metal door that opened when someone came to drag you away for being a bad dog.

'It was in his corner,' Short Hair said.

Pretty Dress looked unsure — then smiled.

'I suppose it was.'

They dropped to their knees to pick up the shiny balls and I hid under the sofa, not daring to open my eyes.

They took forever. When they coaxed me out with a meaty biscuit, I looked at my corner and saw… my bed. All soft and cosy. Just as it should be.

But where was the tree?

That silly, funky tree?

'Come on, boy,' Short Hair said. 'You need a walk.'

As he pulled on his coat, I spotted the tree outside — where trees belong — still covered in shiny balls, looking far prettier than it ever did in the good room.

I looked up and saw Squiggly perched on a branch.

'Nice job,' he called down. 'Now we all get to see it.'

A time to remember how it once felt
A time to regret those who left
A time to sit back and watch
A time to let yourself goA
time to forgive all that often annoys
A time to put others first
A time to endure for the sake of someone you
    love
A time to hold your tongue
A time to laugh at jokes you heard before
A time to not mention uncle Ted might be a
    racist
A time to drink sherry at ten in the morning
A time to hide the Monopoly board
A time to pretend that money is an accept-
    able gift
A time to watch 'Carry on Abroad'
A time to collapse in relief when relatives get
    the hint
... and go
A time to suggest next year in Spain

Merry Christmas from Mo

Husbands

This is a preview from my 2024 novel, 'Husbands'. A peep behind the bright lights and glitter that we think of when we imagine life in Hollywood. A road-trip romcom, of the gayest order.

Fried chicken grease stains my wrinkled white shirt, and undone buttons reveal my pale skin. The world spins as I lean on a pillar in the fancy hotel lobby. My date slips a matte black card into the lift, gesturing for another couple to wait.

As we ride to the penthouse level, he pushes me against the mirrored wall and kisses me hard with lips that taste of whisky.

In the penthouse suite, translucent curtains flutter at windows overlooking garish casino signs lining the strip below.

A bartender with piercing blue eyes pours champagne.

My date is handsome in a craggy, daddy-bear way. Not that I buy into the whole gay men as woodland critters thing. Every online hook-up describes themselves as a bear, an otter, or a pup, and I've yet to find the animal that chimes with what my Spotlight Casting Directory profile calls 'an average build, Hugh Grant type'.

He lifts his glass in a toast. 'Should we hyphenate our last names, or are you taking mine?'

Shit!

I didn't imagine it. There was a wedding chapel, dingy and worn, with stained beige carpeting and rows of plastic chairs. And some campy older guy dressed as Elvis crooning, 'Love Me Tender'. Cheesy organ music played on a loop, and we gave money to a woman who promised our marriage certificate tomorrow. I made jokes about getting it framed to hang in the loo.

'We're not married, though, right?'

He winks. 'I'll call and explain it was a mistake.'

Stressed whispers carry from the other room. I steady myself against the wall as the floor lurches—time to leave. Stop being so polite and so British. Be direct. Tell him to order you a taxi.

'Do you have company?' I say, in the sort of voice my mother might use when asking if the local branch of Waitrose stocks oven chips.

'Just friends.'

The room spins, and my mouth waters. My head is banging, but his hands are on me.

'Shame to waste our honeymoon.' He kisses my neck. 'The bedroom is through there.'

'Yeah, great, but I need the bathroom.'

A door opens at the end of a low-lit hallway, and a guy stands staring. Young. Handsome, with a tiny scar below one eye. Bare-chested. Bold. But mostly young. The floor lurches, and I reach for a wall to steady myself.

His fingers brush my cheek. 'Stay, baby. I'll get you home safe.'

I pull back. 'Call them. Tell them we made a mistake.'

With a grin, he pulls out his phone and pushes a button.

'Siri, remind me to annul the marriage.'

About the Author

I've always believed stories can do two things at once: make you laugh and make you feel less alone. That's what I try to do on every page I write.

I didn't grow up planning to be a novelist — but I grew up needing books. They were my escape, my company, and my way of making sense of the world. Now, I get to create those escapes for other people. My novels explore love, loss, friendship, and the messy, hopeful business of being human.

At the heart of it all is a simple promise: even in life's toughest moments, there's humour, there's connection, and there's always a glimmer of light. That's the world I write about, and I'm thrilled to share it with you.

Also by Mo Fanning

Rainbows and Lollipops

Husbands

Ghosted

Rebuilding Alexandra Small

The Armchair Bride

Plus two short story collections

This is NOT America

This is NOT England